Cattle Valley

Carol Lynne is truly an amazing author and Eye of the Beholder just proves once again what a gift she has...Eye of the Beholder is definitely a five star work and I can not wait to read the next book in the Cattle Valley series ~ *eCata Romance Reviews*

Cattle Valley Days: I love this series and this book is no exception. I can't say enough about how great this series is. If you haven't read them start from the beginning, they're well worth the time and money ~ *Night Owl Romance*

Cattle Valley Days is definitely an "Oh My God!" story that will leave every reader with a need for more. Sizzling storylines, to die for romances and characters that burn up the pages make every novel a five star treat ~ *eCata Romance Reviews*

Carol Lynne proves that literary gay sex does not have to be rough to be exciting, and that love is a universal turn-on ~ *Author, Lisabet Sarai*

Total-E-Bound Publishing books in print from
Carol Lynne:

Campus Cravings Volume One: On the Field
Coach
Side-Lined
Sacking the Quarterback

Campus Cravings Volume Two: Off the Field
Off Season
Forbidden Freshman

Campus Cravings Volume Three: Back on Campus
Broken Pottery
In Bear's Bed

Campus Cravings Volume Four: Dorm Life
Office Advances
A Biker's Vow

Campus Cravings Volume Five: BK House
Hershie's Kiss
Theron's Return

Good-Time Boys
Sonny's Salvation
Garron's Gift
Rawley's Redemption
Twin Temptations

Cattle Valley Volume One
All Play & No Work
Cattle Valley Mistletoe

Cattle Valley Volume Two
Sweet Topping
Rough Ride

Cattle Valley Volume Three
Physical Therapy
Out of the Shadow

Cattle Valley Volume Four
Bad Boy Cowboy
The Sound of White

Cattle Valley Volume Five
Gone Surfin'
The Last Bouquet

Poker Night
Texas Hold 'em
Slow-Play

CATTLE VALLEY
Volume Six

Eye of the Beholder

Cattle Valley Days

CAROL LYNNE

Cattle Valley: Volume Six
ISBN # 978-1-907010-96-5
©Copyright Carol Lynne 2009
Cover Art by April Martinez ©Copyright 2009
Interior text design by Claire Siemaszkiewicz
Total-E-Bound Publishing

EYE OF THE
BEHOLDER

Dedication

For my newest friend Jambrea Jones.
I hope you like this one.

Chapter One

"Watch out!" a familiar voice screamed.

Working on the hay rake, Bo barely had time to turn around before the bull was on him. In a split second decision, he tried to wedge himself between the tines of the rake before the bull had a chance to plough into him and impale him on the steel rods.

Bo screamed as one of the yellow tines plunged into his side, preventing him from hiding further. He covered his head and braced himself for impact. The charging bull didn't stop until he slammed into the machine, mere inches from where Bo stood. The resulting impact not only drove the tine further into Bo's body, but impaled the bull's face as well. The one ton bull pulled back, releasing the tine from his face and tossed his head from side to side, splattering blood all over Bo.

Rance and two of the cowboys finally managed to get lassos around Zero Tolerance's head, but even with three men, they were no match for the strength of the bull.

Trying to remove himself from the rake, Bo felt his flesh begin to rip. "Fuck!" he screamed, his hand immediately going to his side.

Knowing he couldn't go anywhere without injuring himself further, he had no choice but to stand by and watch the three cowboys try to get the prize rodeo bull under control. One thing he could do was call for backup. Moving as little as possible, Bo extracted his cell phone from its holster on his belt and called the main house. Even the slightest movement seemed to drive the tine in deeper. By the time Shep came on the line, Bo was panting through the pain.

"Shep."

"It's Bo. We're gonna need some help out in the east pasture. Zero Tolerance is injured and going nuts. Rance, Buddy and Steve are trying to control him, but they seem to be losing the fight. And call Jeb. If he's in the area, we may be able to save the damned bull."

"We'll be right there."

"Oh, and you might want to bring some rubber gloves from the box in the barn. I'm bleeding like a stuck pig, and I'm gonna need some help getting loose from the hay rake."

"Shit. Should I call an ambulance?"

Bo took a deep breath. His lungs seemed to be fine, but no telling what other internal injuries he may have sustained. Being HIV positive, infections of any kind were always a worry. The blood he could feel running down his side couldn't be good either. "Yeah, I think you'd better. Make sure you give 'em the heads-up on my condition though."

"Will do, hang in there, buddy."

Bo let the phone fall from his bloody hand onto the pasture below. *Goddammit.* He'd been doing so well, not even a single sniffle in the fifteen months he'd been employed.

Reaching down, Bo ripped his T-shirt down the side to get a better look at his injury. Trying to bend down enough to look at the wound, he nearly lost an eye on another of the tines. Sighing, he came to the conclusion he'd be better off just standing as still as possible. He took the tail of the ruined T-shirt and held it against the wound.

Shep, Jeremy and Jim pulled up in the pickup. Shep was the first to jump out, tranquilizer gun in his hand. "Stand back," he ordered.

"Wait," Rance yelled. "He's lost a lot of blood. You could kill him."

Shep looked from Rance to Bo. "Better him than Bo and from the looks of it, if we don't get Bo some help that's exactly what's going to happen."

As soon as Shep fired the tranquilizer dart into the bull, Rance passed his rope off to Jimmy and rushed over to Bo.

"Don't touch me," Bo warned. "I think Shep brought gloves."

Before Rance could turn around, Shep was there, handing out latex gloves to everyone. Gloves on, Shep and Rance approached. Bo knew he looked worse than he was.

"A lot of this belongs to the bull," he explained, gesturing to his blood-splattered face. "My problem's down here on my side. One of the tines seems to be caught on something."

Rance moved to the back of the hay rake and tried to get a better view of what they were dealing with. "I think we're gonna have to disconnect the tine from the machine, then let the doctors remove it from you."

Bo gulped in air, trying his best to overcome the sudden wave of nausea. With his blood continuing to flow at a steady pace from the wound, he knew he wasn't going to remain conscious for much longer. If he were to pass out before Rance worked the tine loose, there was no telling what kind of damage his internal organs would suffer. "Hurry, I don't think I'm gonna last."

"That's enough of that," Rance yelled as he grabbed the tool box and dug around until he found what he needed.

Motioning Shep over, Bo leaned against him. Whispering so Rance wouldn't hear, he spoke in Shep's ear. "I hate to ask you this, but I need you to make sure I stay up on my feet. My vision's starting to get pretty spotty."

Shep wrapped both arms around Bo's chest as Rance worked furiously to free the tine while trying not to move it. Bo laid his head on Shep's shoulder. "I'm sorry, Boss."

"Not your fault. But you owe it to Rance to make it out of this alive, so fight like hell."

"If I don't, tell him…"

"Got it!" Rance yelled. "Get him the hell out of there."

Shep carefully helped Bo move far enough away from the rake to lay him in the soft grass. As Bo struggled to hold onto consciousness, he heard the ambulance's siren. Realising the paramedics would know what to do, Bo allowed himself to close his eyes.

* * * *

Putting on a fresh pair of gloves, Rance knelt beside Bo. "Bo? Wake-up. Come on, open your eyes."

"Let the ambulance through the gate," he yelled at Buddy.

Gently removing the blood-soaked shirt from around the tine, Rance reached down and took off his own western-style shirt. Not wanting to disturb the piece of metal, he held his shirt against the ripped portion of Bo's stomach until Zac Alben tapped him on the shoulder.

Reluctantly, Rance moved out of the way. As Zac and Fire Chief George Manning worked to stabilise and load Bo onto a gurney, Rance was taken back to the previous week.

* * * *

Bo walked into the bunkhouse kitchen in a fantastic mood. "Good morning, all."

Rance glanced up from his plate of bacon and eggs before quickly looking back down. Just the site of the man was enough to drive him crazy, but the cheerful mood and movie star smile were too much. With his shoulder-length black hair still wet from the shower, and water droplets still clinging to the sculpted chest on display, Rance almost groaned at the picture Bo made this early in the morning. He wanted to yell at Bo to button his shirt, but couldn't quite bring himself to do. He must be a sadist.

"What's got you in such a cheery disposition on this fine spring day?" Buddy asked.

"My, my, aren't we using big words today. If you must know, it's one of my favourite days of the year, planting day. The day when all things are possible, and I am a god among mortals. I alone have the power to turn the barren soil into food for man and beasts," Bo explained with his nose in the air.

The entire kitchen erupted in laughter as Rance spotted a wadded napkin sailing through the air, hitting Bo in the face. He attempted to cover his laughter. Despite trying his best to stay away from the walking temptation, Bo was funny as hell and kept them all entertained.

"Watch out for Zero Tolerance. As far as he's concerned you've got a target on your back," Rance mumbled, eating the last of his bacon.

Bo plopped down in the chair beside Rance and shook his head. "What is it with that mean sonofabitch? I've never done a damn thing to that bull, but he seems to go nuts whenever I'm around."

"Maybe he overheard one of your jokes," Rance answered.

Bo leaned over and made exaggerated kissing noises. "You looove my jokes, admit it?"

Pushing his chair back, Rance carried his plate to the sink washing it in the hot soapy water. "I don't know what Zero's beef is with you, but do yourself a favour and give him a wide birth."

"Oh, I get it. Zero. Beef. You're a real funny man."

Shaking his head, Rance lifted his hat off the peg by the door and settled it low on his forehead. "Well, Father Corn, have a wonderful day planting your seed. I'll be up to my shoulders inserting bull sperm into receptive cows. We'll see which one of us feels more like a god by the end of the day."

* * * *

After helping Jeb Garza get Zero Tolerance stitched up and put into one of the holding pens, Rance headed for the hospital in Sheridan. It had been decided soon after Zac assessed Bo's condition that the clinic in Cattle Valley may not be equipped to handle the farmer's injuries.

Despite driving over eighty-five miles an hour the entire way, Rance tried to look casual as he strolled into the emergency room. He spoke to the nurse behind the desk, who told him Bo was in surgery. Armed with the knowledge that at least Bo was still alive, he took the elevator up to the waiting room.

Rance spotted Shep and Jeremy right away and walked towards them. "How is he?"

"He just came out of surgery. They had to remove his spleen and part of his left kidney, but the doctor is optimistic about his recovery."

Rance nodded, trying to absorb the information. "What about his HIV status? Will any of this affect that?"

Shep rubbed the back of his neck. "Not directly, but renal failure is always a concern with HIV patients. With the loss of part of his left kidney, he'll be at higher risk. They'll need to do some adjusting to his current medication regime until he heals, but the doctors think as long as he continues to take care of himself, he should recover nicely."

"I called the guy on his emergency contact card," Jeremy added. "He's flying in from Idaho."

Though he had no right to say anything, Rance didn't like the thought of another man sitting at Bo's bedside. "Who's this guy?"

Jeremy grinned. "Lark's an old friend of Bo's from his days in the commune up north. He and his *partner*, Kade, are the ones who brought Bo to Cattle Valley in the first place."

Rance remembered the first time he'd laid eyes on Bo. It had been in the bakery. He'd been standing in line, when three gorgeous men had entered. He knew immediately they were from out of town. Police work was still in his blood, and he briefly stepped out of line to assess the men.

The small one didn't pose a threat, he knew that right away by the guy's broad smile, but the other two looked almost...dangerous.

What had bothered Rance more than anything was he couldn't keep his eyes off Bo. There was something almost feral about the man's looks that spoke to Rance's cock, instead of his brain. He hated the feeling and left the bakery soon after.

He gathered the two men coming into town were the same two who had been with Bo that day. Rance didn't know a lot about Bo's life before hiring on at the Back Breaker, but he'd heard plenty of rumours about the free-love-type commune he'd lived on in Canada. What if the three of them had been lovers?

"So when will these friends get here?" he asked.

Jeremy looked at his watch. "In about an hour. Why? You volunteering to pick them up from the airport?"

He hadn't been, but he knew if he declined, he'd look like an ass. "Sure."

* * * *

With his arms crossed over his chest, Rance waited for Lark and Kade by the arrivals exit. It was going on nine o'clock and his stomach was reminding him that he hadn't eaten since breakfast. He thought about stopping someplace to eat on the way back to the hospital, but Rance wasn't sure if he could be in the company of Bo's friends that long without asking questions he had no business asking.

He spotted the big biker-looking guy first and held up his hand to signal him. The smaller one, Lark, by the description he'd been given, stepped out of the biker's shadow and headed towards Rance. He'd heard Bo talk about the two men coming towards him for a year, so why did he suddenly feel nervous?

"How is he?" Lark asked, adjusting the big backpack on his shoulder.

"Out of surgery and stable when I left the hospital. I'll fill you both in on the drive over." He held out his hand. "Name's Rance, by the way."

Lark shook his hand before gesturing to the big guy. "I'm Lark and this is my partner, Kade. It's nice to finally put a face with a name."

Rance was surprised to hear Bo had talked about him by name to Lark. He wondered what he'd said.

He noticed Kade was more standoffish than Lark, not even bothering to shake Rance's hand. Well that was fine with him. He didn't need to play nice with these two guys, he was simply doing Bo a favour by picking them up.

"Is that all the luggage you have?" Rance gestured towards the large duffle slung over Kade's broad shoulder.

"That's it. Lark has to fly back on Sunday. He's got final exams next week. And I don't need more than a change of jeans and a couple T-shirts."

Rance turned towards the door and rolled his eyes. He hadn't asked the man for an inventory of his luggage. He'd learned one thing, though. Kade would evidently be staying on at least through the following week. *Shit.*

After digging his keys out of his pocket, Rance pointed towards the ranch pickup. He didn't say a word as Kade threw the duffel and Lark's backpack into the bed and climbed in beside him. At least Lark sat in the middle. Rance didn't know that he'd survive the cold chill coming from Kade on the drive over.

As soon as he pulled out of the parking lot, the questions began. Rance tried his best to explain everything he'd learned from talking to Shep.

"I haven't talked directly to the doctor, so don't quote me on any of this," Rance added.

"How long do they think it'll take him to recover?" Kade asked.

"He should feel a lot better in three to four weeks, but he won't be completely healed for at least eight."

"How will it affect his job? This Shep guy doesn't plan on hiring someone to take his place, does he?" Kade asked.

"We haven't really talked about it. Bo's the only farmer we have on payroll and he'd only just begun to plant the crops, so I'm not sure what Shep will want to do."

"I can do it," Lark piped up. "I spent the first eighteen years of my life around farming."

"You've got a week left of school," Kade reminded him.

"Yeah, but I can do as much as possible until I have to leave Sunday night, and then finish up once finals are over." Lark started kissing Kade's neck. "Come on, it'll be a fun way to spend the summer. We'd planned on moving to Cattle Valley anyway, we'll just move the date up a few months."

"And what am I supposed to do while you're off playing farmer-boy?" Kade asked, tickling Lark's ribs.

Laughing, Lark swatted Kade's hands. "You can build me that cabin you're always going on and on about."

Rance saw his opening and took it. "I'm afraid you won't have much luck in that department. Available land around Cattle Valley is pretty scarce."

"We'll figure something out," Kade added, kissing the top of Lark's blond head.

Crap.

* * * *

It was almost three days before they allowed Bo to have regular visitors. Of course Lark got to see him right away, but evidently Rance didn't rate as high. Yeah, he was bitter, and took it out on everyone around him, especially his cowhands.

After taking a shower to clean off the stink, Rance dressed in his new jeans and black western snap-front shirt. He placed his black Stetson low on his forehead, as usual, and grabbed the keys from the desk beside the front door.

"You going to see Bo?" Steve hollered from the barn.

"Yep."

"Give him our best. And tell him things are boring around here without him," Steve chuckled.

"Will do," Rance answered, getting into his big black four-wheel drive truck.

Before driving into Sheridan, he stopped at Brynn's Bakery and picked up one of Bo's favourite cinnamon rolls. He wasn't sure if he could eat it yet, but if he knew Bo, he'd sure as hell try to get away with it.

He hated to admit it to himself, but he was really looking forward to seeing the farmer again. How many times had he wished Bo had never stepped foot in Cattle Valley?

Rance shook his head. He knew it had nothing to do with the man himself and everything to do with the way Bo made him feel. Once upon a time he would've jumped on Bo right there in the bakery that first day and staked his claim, but he wasn't the same man as back then, and never would be.

He chuckled to himself. No matter what he said to the man, Bo never seemed to give up trying to get into Rance's jeans. If Bo only knew how much Rance would enjoy just that, but his pride wouldn't allow it. Better to give Bo the fantasy of the way things could be instead of the reality Rance would give him.

Before he knew it, he was boarding the elevator up to Bo's room, the bag containing the cinnamon roll clutched in his hand. The floor seemed pretty quiet until he neared Bo's room. He heard Bo's customary laugh and his chest tightened. Yeah, he'd missed the silly sonofabitch.

Knocking on the door frame, he took his hat off and tried his best to smooth his black hair. Bo was surrounded by people. From the looks of it, Kade had taken up residence in the big chair beside Bo's bed. Shep, Jeremy and a couple of the hands from the EZ Does It were also there.

No one in the room seemed to be aware of Rance's entrance. He almost set the bag on the counter and left, but then loud-mouth Logan Miller spotted him.

"Hey, look what the cat drug in!"

The small crowd around Bo parted, and Rance got his first look at the man since his accident. His heart sunk as he took in the large piece of homemade pie Bo was devouring. *So much for a store-bought cinnamon roll.*

"Hey, you," Bo said around a mouthful of food. "'Bout time you got in here to see me."

Rance stepped forward and set the white sack on Bo's bedside table. "They wouldn't let me in before now."

He thought he detected some unspoken emotion in Bo's face at the statement. Bo's gaze slid to Kade before returning to Rance. "What'd ya bring me?"

Rance shrugged. "Nothing much. I happened to stop in at Brynn's, so I brought you a roll."

Bo licked his lips. "Thanks. Sorry, but I've just eaten two pieces of Jax's homemade apple pie. I'm sure I'll get to it before the day is through, though."

"No big deal," Rance said.

"Well, we'd better take off." Shep reached out to lay a hand on Bo's shoulder.

"Yeah, we need to get going, too," Jax added. "Logan's working on a bike that's giving him fits, and the guy isn't known for his patience."

Shep chuckled. "Nate's bike again, I guess?"

Logan shook his head. "Every time I turn around the man wants something else added to it. I told him he should just have himself a custom job made, but he said he doesn't like to wait long enough to have one built for him."

Everyone in the room who knew Nate laughed. Their new mayor was a fantastic guy, but a bit spoiled when it came to waiting for anything.

Bo said goodbye to his friends, and they filtered out into the hall, one by one. Rance hoped Kade would also leave, but no such luck.

"Get over here and have a seat," Bo beckoned, patting the bed beside him.

"I don't think that's a good idea," Kade cut in, staring daggers at Rance.

Bo glanced at Kade and shook his head. "Do me a favour and go ask the nurse when I can have another pain pill."

"You still have over an hour," Kade replied.

"Well. Go. Ask. Anyway." Bo's voice left no room for misunderstanding. He wanted Kade gone.

With a disgusted sound erupting from his throat, Kade stood and left the room. Rance watched the big guy go and turned back to Bo.

"Geeze, why does that guy hate me so much?"

Studying Rance, Bo sighed. "Because I like you so much."

"And what, he has his own designs on you?" Rance asked, sitting at the foot of Bo's bed with his hat beside him.

Bo chuckled, holding his side. "You know it hurts when I laugh, right?"

"Sorry. I wasn't trying to be funny."

"Well it was funny. Kade doesn't have eyes for anyone but Lark. Nope, Kade's problem is that he thinks you don't want me because of my positive status. See, he's got HIV, too."

"You being positive has nothing to do with the reason I won't hop into your bed," Rance informed Bo.

"Really? Then what's the reason you won't let me at that nice package you're carrying? Especially since you've gone to all the trouble of looking absolutely drool-worthy today?"

Rance's gaze swung to the window. "Personal reasons."

No way would he unload his story on the man beside him. Shep knew about his past, but that was only because he'd gotten drunk one night and confessed. Nope, it wouldn't do either of them any good to travel down memory lane. Bo was the kind of man that would claim it was no big deal, but Rance knew first hand how big a deal it really was.

A warm hand covered his, snapping Rance out of his thoughts. He glanced down at Bo's hand, IV still connected. Pity was one thing he couldn't stand.

"Don't feel sorry for me," Rance bristled, pulling his hand out from under Bo's.

"I don't. At least not for whatever reason you think. I do feel sorry that you don't believe in me enough to give me a chance."

"I told you, it has nothing to do with you." Rance stood, placing his hat back on his head. "When're you gettin' out of here?"

"Two more days," Bo mumbled, refusing to make eye contact.

"I can move you into my house if you think you'd be more comfortable during your recovery. Lord knows it's a hell of a lot quieter than the bunkhouse."

"I'll let you know. Lark and Kade have offered to let me stay with them. They rented Casey's old house next door to the church until they can find their own place."

The news caused a pain in Rance's chest. "Whatever. Just let me know so I can change the sheets in the spare bedroom."

Rance left the room without a backward glance. It was probably better that Bo's friends took care of him.

So why did the idea hurt so much?

Chapter Two

By the third week in the tiny rental house, Bo was going nuts. He'd done so many crossword puzzles he thought he might be ready for Jeopardy. As he watched Lark get ready for another day of farming, his jealousy boiled over.

"Just take me out to the ranch for the day," he begged.

"And then what?" Lark asked. "I know you. You won't be able to sit by and watch everyone else work, without feeling the need to get your hands dirty."

"Come on, even if I do nothing but sit on the porch, it'll be better than staring at these same old walls all day."

Lark put a hand on his hip and narrowed his eyes. "You'll wear sandals. I know you wouldn't dare do any work without proper shoes."

Bo readily agreed. It didn't take boots to roam around and shoot the shit with the other guys. Mostly he wanted to see Rance. He hadn't spoken to him since the day the foreman had visited him in the hospital. Even if it was self-torture, Bo needed a fix of those dark-brown eyes, that heavenly ass and broadly muscled chest. And if he got a peek of those lickable dimples, well then, more's the better.

Wearing an old pair of cargo shorts, and an even older red Genesis concert T-shirt, Bo stuffed his feet into a pair of flip-flops and packed his lunch. He was down to one pain pill a day, so thought he would be fine away from the house. If he got tired, he could always lay down on his bed in the bunkhouse.

Bo was also hoping to talk to Shep about coming back to work several hours a day to enter planting data into the computer. He may not be up to the physical work of a farmer, but he could sure as hell sit his ass in a chair and type.

"Ready?" Lark asked, coming out of the bedroom where Kade was still asleep.

"Hell yeah, been ready."

Lark laughed and grabbed the lunch he'd made himself earlier. "Kade said he'd be around town later, so if you want to come home before I'm finished for the day, just give him a call."

"Is he going to work at Logan's shop again?" Kade and Logan had become fast friends, and lately Kade had been spending most of his day working alongside his new friend on motorcycles.

"Probably, but he's also got a meeting with someone about some land. He heard of a couple of older guys who were considering moving further south. I guess one of them has been having some breathing trouble."

Bo tried to think of anyone in Cattle Valley who fit that description. "You're not talking about Ben Zook, are you?"

Lark shrugged. "I don't know the guy's name."

They got into the small hybrid SUV that Lark called a car, and headed towards the Back Breaker. As they passed the bakery, Bo thought of the gift Rance had brought him that day he'd visited. Even though Rance made it seem like the gesture was no big deal, Bo knew better. Despite all his huffing and puffing, Rance liked him.

"I think it's time I moved back out to the ranch," he informed Lark.

"Why? Am I getting on your nerves that bad?" Lark chuckled.

"No, but the noises coming from your bedroom at night are enough to make a guy feel like a voyeur. Especially when that guy hasn't had sex in over a year." It was hard for Bo to believe he'd gone an entire year without fuckin' or being fucked. Up until he moved to Cattle Valley his whole life had seemed to revolve around his dick.

Lark's face went red. "Shit. Why didn't you say something before?"

"Would you have invited me in?" he asked smoothly, sliding his hand to Lark's thigh.

"Stop that," Lark laughed and slapped Bo's hand.

"It was worth a shot." Bo knew very well what Lark looked like while getting fucked. Hell, he'd done it enough times he knew every freckle on Lark's body intimately, but that had been several years ago. Lark had turned eighteen and left the commune for the university in Idaho where he'd met Kade.

Bo didn't hold any grudges. Life on the commune was a hell of a lot different than anywhere else he'd ever lived. Oh, that reminded him.

"Have you talked to your folks lately?"

Lark squirmed in his seat. "Not for a couple weeks. They're not happy I'm working on the farm down here instead of taking my turn at Sunrise Gardens. Why?"

"I think something's going on with Jan, but I can't get anyone to give me a straight answer. Every time I call up there, she's either busy or not there."

"That's weird. What do you need to talk to her about?" Lark asked.

"I want her to sign the damn divorce papers I sent up there almost a year ago."

"No shit? I thought for sure you were a free man by now."

"I wish. It hasn't really mattered because it's not like I'm dating anyway. But if Rance ever does give me a chance, I'd like to be free and clear. Start things between us off on the right foot, ya know?"

"You want me to give Mom a call later, see if I can weasel anything out of her?"

"If you wouldn't mind." Bo took an apple out of his lunch cooler and bit into it, juice running down his chin. "Damn these are good. I'm gonna have to get me some more of 'em."

"We'll swing by the store on the way home. The way you and Kade go through fruit, you'd think the two of you were vegetarians."

"Nope, just two guys who know the importance of staying healthy." It didn't matter what he did during any given day, his HIV status was never far from his thoughts, especially now. If eating his weight in fresh fruits and vegetables allowed him to live another year or so, it was worth it.

They pulled into the Back Breaker and Lark parked next to the row of pickups. "Ever feel this car is out of place here?"

Lark laughed. "Yep, but every time I get gas I thank my lucky stars I don't drive one of these guzzlers. The first thing I'm gonna do once I get a real job is buy a Prius."

Bo held his side as he climbed out of the small car. "That sounds like a perfect car for you, but I can't really see Kade driving it."

"Probably not, but he'll either learn to adapt or freeze his nuts off in the winter trying to ride that damn Harley."

As they neared the barn, Lark waved. "I'll see ya later. Should be finished around five."

"Sound's good." Bo continued on to the barn, anxious to see Rance.

Buddy was the first guy he ran in to. They stood and talked shit for a few minutes before Rance appeared. Clad in his customary well-fitting jeans and black T-shirt.

"Don't you have work to do, Buddy?" Rance asked.

"Sure thing, Boss." Steve tipped his hat to Rance and shot Bo a wink. "Nice to see ya again."

"Same here." Bo turned to Rance after Buddy walked out of the barn. "You got a burr in your britches?"

Rance turned back towards the ranch office. "The only pain in my ass around here is you."

Bo rolled his eyes and followed the foreman. It seemed Rance was back to his old self. Without an invitation, Bo sat in one of the old chairs in the office and put his bare feet up on Rance's desk. If he doubted the beauty of any part of his body, it certainly wasn't his feet.

Rance tossed his hat onto the file cabinet and stared at Bo's position. "What the hell're you doing?"

"Waiting for you to be civil," Bo answered, resting his hands on his chest.

"Get your feet off the desk."

Bo flexed his perfectly shaped toes. "Why, don't you like feet?"

Rance picked up a pen and jabbed the soft arch of Bo's foot.

"Ouch." Bo jerked his feet back, hurting his side with the sudden movement.

"Fuck!" he yelled, hand going to his healing scar.

"Shit, I'm sorry," Rance said, jumping up from his chair to kneel beside Bo. "You okay? Do I need to call someone?"

Bo gazed into Rance's black eyes. The lips he'd been waiting over a year to kiss were right there. Unable to stop himself, Bo leaned forward, sealing his mouth over Rance's. When Rance didn't move, Bo prodded the soft lips with his tongue.

With a soft groan, Rance opened and suddenly Bo's tongue was exploring the foreman's mouth. Reaching out, Bo clasped a hand to the back of Rance's neck and pulled him closer as Rance began to kiss him back.

Fuck. Bo was in heaven. He slid off the chair and knelt in front of Rance, pulling the man into his arms. God this felt right.

Rance moaned again and began fucking Bo's mouth with his tongue. It was hotter than the Fourth of July. Bo felt the bulge behind Rance's fly press against him. Not one to waste an opportunity, Bo reached down and blatantly groped the erection trapped in Rance's jeans.

Like a light switch being turned off, Rance pulled back and shot to his feet. He grabbed his hat, settled it on his head and left the office without a single word being said.

Bo was left on his knees with a bull-sized hard-on. What the fuck had just happened?

* * * *

As soon as he was safely shut in his house, Rance let loose. Tossing his beloved hat onto the hardwood floor he kicked the sofa.

"Sonofabitch!" he cursed himself, falling to his knees.

He'd fought his attraction to Bo too goddamn long to end up making such a stupid mistake.

In a fit of anger, he raised his fist over his head and slammed it against his crotch. In the split second his hand connected with his still semi-hard cock, the air whooshed out of Rance's lungs.

Falling to his side, he cupped his hands over his groin and drew up his legs. *Jesus!* It felt like his stomach was trying to force its way out of his mouth as the pain continued to reverberate up from his dick.

He spit several times on the floor before the bile finally made an appearance. All he could think about as he emptied the contents of his stomach onto the hardwood was thank god he didn't have carpeting.

Once the nausea had passed, Rance managed to roll far enough in the opposite direction so that he was away from the stench. As he laid there crying like a baby, memories of Oren Reynolds rushed him from all sides.

Their first meeting in the diner down the street from the station, the subsequent dates where he tried his best to woo the small blond man into his bed. The first night they'd made love, oh god, what a night that had been. The man had been like no lover he'd ever had. Though small in stature, he'd been an absolute animal in the sack. Whoever said accountants were boring, hadn't known Oren.

With his balls swollen and bruised, thoughts of Oren made Rance hard. Even if it weren't for his extra baggage, the fact that he was still being haunted by a ghost made a relationship with Bo impossible.

No, that wasn't exactly the truth. Oren wasn't a real ghost, hell, the man wasn't even dead. The last time he'd seen him had been in the courtroom, perched on the witness stand, confessing every detail of his love life with Rance to a jury and a roomful of people.

It had been impossible for Rance to stay in Boston after that. His face had been plastered on the front page of every newspaper in the state, and a few national papers as well.

Packing up and coming out to Cattle Valley had been the best decision he'd ever made, away from Oren, away from the public speculation. Here he was just Rance and that's the way he needed it to stay.

Exposing his shame to Bo wasn't an option, so his dick had better well cooperate.

* * * *

After the shock of Rance's sudden departure had worn off, Bo went in search of Shep. He didn't see him in or around the pens, so he made his way to the main house. He held a hand to his side as he slowly climbed the porch steps. It wouldn't do for his boss to see him in any kind of discomfort.

He rang the bell and waited. When no one came to the door right away, Bo took a seat on the porch swing in the shade. He figured if Shep was inside, most likely he was busy doing morning stuff with Jeremy, and who the hell could blame him?

Maybe he should forget Rance and find himself a young stud in town. Perhaps a couple of meaningless tumbles would cure him of the ache in his shorts. Too bad he loved the sonofabitch. Bo knew it served him right. After fucking anything, male or female that walked, maybe it was karma's way of biting him in the ass.

He was still pondering karma and her bitchy attitude when Shep poked his head out the door. "Thought I heard someone out here earlier."

Bo grinned. "Quite alright, I figured you must be...busy and decided to make myself comfortable."

Shep sat in a chair opposite the swing. "How're you feeling?"

"Better. Bored mostly. The doctor said I can't do anything strenuous for another four weeks, but I was hoping I could talk you into letting me do some of the computer work."

Shep looked at him like he was crazy. "Hasn't Rance been paying ya every week? I gave him specific instructions…"

"Yeah, he has," Bo cut Shep off before he got Rance in trouble. "It's just that I'm not very good at sittin' around."

"So take a vacation. I swear I'm not trying to get rid of you, but there isn't enough non-physical work to keep you busy and I know you. If you're around work that needs doin' you'll step in and try to do it. My insurance company would go ape shit if they found out."

Bo ran his hands through his shoulder-length dark brown hair. "I guess I could take a trip to Sunrise Gardens and get my damn divorce papers from my ex-wife."

"See? Perfect. Take a nice trip and then come home ready to work."

The screen door opened and Jeremy came out, feet and torso bare. "Oh, hey, Bo."

"Hey," he returned, trying not to stare at the leanly muscled chest on display.

"Just hanging out?" Jeremy asked, taking a seat on Shep's lap.

"Had to get out of the cracker box Lark and Kade are renting. You hear anything about Ben Zook moving down south?"

"No, but it doesn't surprise me. Living at the base of the mountain like they do, they really get dumped on in the winter. I imagine it's a lot for two older guys to keep up with."

Bo nodded his head. "Lark said Kade was going to look at their place. He said the guys were moving south because of asthma problems."

Shep nodded. "Yeah, it sounds like them alright. I'll be sorry to see old Ben leave town, but at least it's good news for your friends."

"Kade's drawn up some dream cabin he's promised to build Lark. I guess at least if there's already a house on the land they won't be living in a tent while Kade builds it."

"Make sure he talks to Hal."

"Oh, they've already been talking. Kade's hot to get the project started."

"I still don't know much about Kade, but Lark's been a damn fine worker while you've been laid up."

For some reason, Bo felt an ounce of pride at the compliment. "Lark's a hell of a farmer. He taught me damn near everything I know, been doing it since he was old enough to walk."

Out of the corner of his eye, Bo watched Rance enter the barn. He must not have been as nonchalant as he'd hoped.

"Still no progress?" Shep asked.

"Huh?"

Shep tipped his head towards the barn. "I figured with the accident and all, the two of you would've finally come to terms with stuff."

Bo grunted and shook his head. "I can't figure him out. I kissed him earlier and at first everything seemed fine. He was in fact, very receptive until I guess I went a little too far. Then it was like being dumped over the head with a bucket of cold water." Bo sighed. "I don't know what to do anymore."

The telephone inside the house began to ring and Shep gave Jeremy's butt a playful slap. "Let me up, love. I'm expecting a call from the PBR."

Jeremy stood and Shep raced inside to catch the phone. After staring at the barn for several moments, Jeremy headed towards the door. "I don't exactly know what happened to Rance in Boston, but it was enough to drive him here."

Bo nodded, as Jeremy opened the door.

"Seems to me the internet might be a good place to go for answers," Jeremy mumbled before closing the screen door.

Chapter Three

Bo was kicked back in the overstuffed easy chair watching a baseball game. Kade was cuddled on the couch with Lark, who had his nose buried in a TA Chase novel on his e-reader. The boner pushing against the front of Lark's sweats told Bo it must be a good one.

He'd been battling back and forth with himself all afternoon. As much as he wanted to know what Rance's problem was, it felt like an invasion of the man's privacy. "Can I ask you a question?"

Neither man looked up from what they were doing. "Helloooo."

Lark eventually looked up from his e-reader. "What?"

"I wanted to ask you guys your opinion on something."

Lark nudged Kade until he took his eyes away from the television screen. "Bo needs to ask us something," Lark told him.

When he had both their attention, he suddenly didn't know where to start. "Uh...let's say you wanted to find something out about someone. Would it be wrong to search for answers about them on the internet?"

"Yes," Lark quickly said.

"No," Kade answered at the same time.

The two men looked at each other. Lark's eyes narrowed. "I can't believe you just said that."

"Why? If it's on the internet it's like free information. What's wrong with looking it up?" Kade attempted to defend himself.

"Because, we both know he's talking about Rance. And I happen to think it would be wrong to go behind his back. I'm sure if Rance wanted Bo to know his past, he'd tell him."

"But he hasn't." Kade's voice started to rise.

Bo had been around the two men enough to know to get out of the way if they were about to argue. First there was screaming, then came the fucking, neither of which he felt like listening to.

"Maybe there's a reason he hasn't," Lark continued, hands on his hips.

Even though the two of them were staring daggers at each other, Bo noticed the front of Lark's sweats were more tented than ever. *Oh, boy.*

Standing, he pointed towards the door. "I'm just gonna grab a few things and spend the night at the ranch. Give you two time alone."

He doubted either of the men even heard him as they continued the argument. Bo quickly threw a change of clothes into his duffle and picked up Lark's keys on the way out. "You'll have to have Kade give you a lift out to the ranch in the morning. Sorry."

Throwing the duffle into the passenger seat, he headed out.

If such a simple question could elicit such a strong reaction from the pair of love birds currently pulling each other's feathers out back at the house, it pretty much gave him his answer. Nope. Despite the temptation, he would not dig into Rance's personal life. At least not on the internet, but that didn't mean he wouldn't try and get something out of the man himself.

He pulled into the ranch yard and parked beside Rance's truck. Noticing the foreman's lights were still on, he decided there was no time like the present. He may end up making an enemy after all was said and done, but at least he'd be able to move on.

Climbing the porch steps he knocked on the screen door. It took a few moments, but he thought he heard Rance call out. Opening the door, he took a step inside. "Rance?"

"Back here."

Bo followed the voice to the bedroom. Covered only by a sheet, Rance was lying in bed with a bottle of Jack Daniels in one hand and an ice bag held to his nuts in the other.

"What happened?" Bo asked.

Rance looked his way and groaned. "Go away."

"Are you hurt?" Bo asked, sitting on the edge of the bed.

"Dammit, I said go away," Rance slurred, obviously drunk.

Taking the near empty bottle of whisky out of Rance's hand, Bo set it on the table. Gesturing towards the ice pack he asked. "Get kicked?"

"No," Rance answered, slinging his arm over his eyes. "Go back to your friends, Bo."

The command hurt. "Funny, I thought you were my friend."

"Well you thought wrong. Now give me back my whisky, and leave me the hell alone," Rance slurred.

Bo studied Rance for a few moments. Was this the result of that single kiss? "What the fuck happened to you to make you into such a cold bastard?" he wondered aloud.

Rance uncovered his eyes and stared at Bo. "You came to town."

"What's that supposed to mean? All I ever wanted from you was love and affection. The same goddamn thing everyone wants. You want it too. I see it in your eyes when you look at me, so why all the drama?"

Rance's voice turned sarcastic. "I don't need those things and I don't need you. Go find someone else to fuck."

Bo stood and handed Rance back the bottle of Jack. "Yeah, maybe you're right. Maybe I have wasted my time falling for you. I just thought...hell, forget it."

Bo walked out of Rance's bedroom without a backward glance. He grabbed his duffle from the car and went in to the bunkhouse. Steve, Buddy and Jim had on the same baseball game Kade had been watching.

"Who's winning?" he asked, making himself comfortable on one end of the couch.

"Mariners," Steve answered. Noticing the duffle he'd dropped on his way in the door, Steve gestured. "That mean you're back?"

"Guess so. I need to make a run up to Canada to take care of some personal business, but it seems you guys are stuck with me again."

Buddy stretched out his leg and nudged Bo's thigh. "Good to have you back, man."

"Thanks."

* * * *

Bo pulled into the small parking lot outside the gates of Sunrise Gardens and turned off the ignition. He hoped he was doing the right thing. Unannounced visitors were frowned upon, but Bo hoped the years he'd spent working the farm would smooth his way.

Getting out of the rental car, he grabbed his bag out of the backseat and walked to the guard shack.

"Well I'll be a two-headed toad. Bo Lawson, what brings you here?" Randy asked, slapping Bo on the back.

"Came to see everyone and pick up the divorce papers from Jan."

Randy's face paled. "Uh, does Jan know you're coming?"

What the fuck? "No, Jan doesn't know I'm coming. Why? Is there a problem?"

Bo could tell by the way his old friend was behaving that there was indeed a problem. His resolve to see his estranged wife rose to new heights.

"I'm not sure. Hold on while I call Jim."

Randy disappeared into the small guard building and picked up the phone. The fact that Randy was calling Jim wasn't anything out of the ordinary. As co-owner of Sunrise Gardens, nothing happened without Jim's say so. He held his breath, waiting for Randy to finish the call.

"Jim'll be down to pick you up in a minute," Randy told him.

"Thanks."

Instead of opening the big gates, Randy unlocked the walk-in gate and allowed Bo to pass. It didn't escape Bo's notice that Randy had cut-off the small talk between them. He wasn't sure what Jim had told Randy, but it appeared he was following the boss's orders.

Bo tossed his bag to the ground and waited. Within ten minutes he spotted the golf cart buzzing his way. Jim pulled up along side of Bo and hopped out of the cart. Bo was customarily wrapped in Jim's loving embrace.

"How're you feeling?" Jim asked, stepping back to look Bo up and down.

Bo knew Lark had told his father about the farm accident. He rested his hand against the healing scar and nodded. "A hell of a lot better. I should be able to return to work in a few weeks."

"Good, glad to hear it." Jim pulled Bo back into his arms once again and kissed him.

It wasn't the kind of kiss you gave a friend, no, this was a kiss for a past lover. Hell, Bo had been a lover to most of the men and women who lived in Sunrise Gardens. Accepting Jim's playful tongue came naturally to Bo and he felt himself getting hard.

Jim obviously noticed it too. Pulling back, Jim ran a hand over the front of Bo's jeans. "Been a while."

"That it has," Bo agreed.

A large part of him wanted to bend Jim over the golf cart and fuck his brains out. He knew from past experience that Jim would welcome his entrance, but Bo needed answers first.

Staring Jim in the eyes, he asked the question he'd come to ask. "What's going on with Jan?"

Jim didn't look surprised by the question, just uncomfortable. "Let's get you up to the house and get you settled. We can talk there."

Giving his old friend the courtesy he deserved, Bo nodded and tossed his duffle in the back of the cart.

As they made their way to the small town Jim and his wife Lynda had established, Bo breathed in. He could smell the rich soil in the air. After years spent planting crops on the commercial-grade organic farm, Bo knew most of the fields had already been seeded.

Though Jim and Lynda hadn't set out to establish one of the countries most prosperous farms, it had definitely been an added benefit. Now their compound of free-loving residents could live the life they chose, while making enough money to live quite comfortably.

As he rode through town, Bo waved to several old friends. Monogamy wasn't a word used in Sunrise Gardens. Here, sex was sex, and everyone enjoyed the pleasant pastime with whoever they chose, regardless of their marital status.

Instead of driving to the house, Jim pulled up in front of the micro-brewery. "Care for a drink first?"

Bo nodded. "Yeah, I get the feeling I'm going to need it."

Entering the bar was like stepping back into his old life. How many evenings had he spent groping some random lover in that very room?

Shaking his head, Bo chuckled at himself. He'd only been in town for five minutes and sex was already forefront in his mind. Although it had been over a year since he'd fucked or been fucked, Bo didn't think he missed the place. The reason he'd left in the first place was because he yearned for something more than a daily dose of sex. Even his marriage to Jan hadn't been one of true love, which was how Lark and Kade had convinced him to move to Cattle Valley.

"You okay?" Jim asked, passing him a beer.

"Yeah. Just a lot of old memories in this place."

"Some of them good, I hope," Jim winked.

"Depends on your definition of good, I guess."

Jim, Lynda and their third partner, Neil were the exception to the norm in Sunrise Gardens. Although they enjoyed sex with others, there was actually a true and lasting love between them. That's what Bo had been after the most. He wanted to make love with a partner, not just fuck him.

"What's going on in that head of yours?" Jim asked, covering Bo's hand with his own.

Turning his hand over, Bo threaded his fingers through Jim's. "Karma, I guess. Here I had all the sex a man could ask for, but none of the true love I craved. Now I have the love I craved, but none of the sex."

Jim squeezed Bo's hand. "Yeah, that Karma's a bitch. Lark told me about Rance. Sorry to hear he still hasn't come around."

Bo should've known Lark would spill the beans to his dad. "Maybe I want too much. I mean, I'm not exactly the catch of the century. Maybe sex is all I'm destined to have."

"Bullshit. I don't believe that and neither do you."

Bo leaned in and thrust his tongue into Jim's mouth. He knew, even as he sucked on Jim's tongue, that he was doing it more for comfort than anything else, but he was so tired of feeling alone.

Jim fisted Bo's shoulder-length hair in his hands and straddled his lap without ever breaking the kiss. It was easy to feel Jim's passion as it ground against Bo's torso. Bo almost threw caution to the wind and let the man on his lap have exactly what he was after, but he'd come to Sunrise Gardens for a bigger purpose.

Breaking the kiss, he put his hands on Jim's gyrating hips to still him. "We need to talk."

A look passed over Jim's face and Bo knew the man had been trying to distract him. "What are you so afraid to tell me that you'd let me fuck you right here in a public place?"

Jim slowly rose and settled himself back in his chair. After a few drinks of his beer, he stared Bo straight in the eyes. "Jan's dying."

Bo didn't know what he expected to hear, but it definitely wasn't that. He felt momentarily paralysed by the news. Jan had been a young, healthy woman when he'd left, or at least he thought so. He remembered the phone calls they'd shared after he'd moved to Cattle Valley. Something had been off, even then, but he chalked it up to the way he'd left. A thought occurred to him as his gut clenched. "I didn't make her sick…did I?"

"No!" Jim was quick to say. Finishing his beer in one gulp, he signalled for another. "I don't know how to even begin to tell you this…"

"Tell me."

"She had a baby six months ago…a boy."

What? That would mean she was pregnant when Bo left her. "Is he mine?"

Jim shook his head. "No, but the birth taxed her already malformed heart. She's at the hospital in Regina."

"Excuse me," Bo said, getting up from the table and walking towards the restroom.

Turning the faucet on, Bo splashed water on his face. Staring at himself in the mirror, he tried to comprehend what he'd learned. He wondered why Jan hadn't told him about the baby. Had she known having the child would kill her?

One of the reasons Bo had agreed to marry Jan in the first place was because she had made it perfectly clear she didn't want children. With his HIV status, fathering a child wasn't an option he could live with, so it had seemed like the ideal marriage for both of them.

Bowing his head, he braced his arms on the sides of the sink and allowed the tears to come. Whether the boy was his or not, he would've never left her had he known. Maybe that's why she hadn't told him? Did she get together with the baby's father after he left?

The door opened and Jim stepped into the small room. "You okay?"

"Why didn't anyone tell me?"

"Jan begged us not to."

"Why?"

Jim crossed his arms and leaned back against the sink beside Bo. "I'm not sure, but I have my theories."

"And they are?"

"You're still technically married. When she dies, you not only get custody of Joey, but her life insurance as well. Maybe she was trying to make things easier for you?"

Bo exploded. "Easier? What? I was supposed to get a phone call saying my wife was dead, and oh, by the way, you have a child to take care of?"

Jim put his hands on Bo's shoulders. "It's an ugly situation all around, but the important thing is that child. He'll need you."

Bo chuckled. "Yeah, right. I've never been needed in my entire life. I wouldn't know how to deal with it."

Shaking his head, he gazed pleadingly at Jim. "Isn't there someone else? Who's the biological father?"

"He's not in the picture, never has been. Some guy Jan took a shine to when she went into Winnepeg for that concert."

Bo remembered. He'd sent her off with her girlfriends with a smile on his face, glad she was getting out of Sunrise Gardens for a few days. Shit. "What about someone else here in town? Surely there's someone who's grown attached to the boy."

"Sure, Lynda's fallen completely in love with the little guy, but I think you need to think long and hard about it. You're still in shock. Give yourself some time to get used to the idea."

Taking hold of Bo's hand, Jim gave him a little tug towards the door. "Would you like to meet him?"

Bo wiped the drying tears from his cheeks. Did he dare? He thought of his life in Cattle Valley. He didn't even own a house. He supposed the life insurance would take care of that, but was he even equipped to raise a child? What if he got sick?

"Come on. Don't think too much right now. Meet Joey and take things from there."

Bo nodded and allowed Jim to lead him out of the restroom.

The ride to Jim's house was one of the longest of Bo's life. How long had it been since he'd even held a baby? *Fuck. Have I ever?* He'd practically grown up on the streets of St. Louis after his whore of a mother had brought one too many tricks home.

Bo shoved thoughts of his mother away. He'd learned long ago questioning a mother's love never got him anywhere but depressed.

Jim pulled up in front of the house. "You ready for this?"

"No, but I'm not sure that I'll ever be ready."

Bo climbed the steps and followed Jim into the house. He was enveloped immediately in a bear hug. Neil, the third member of Jim and Lynda's ménage family gave him the customary welcome kiss. Bo returned the kiss politely, but didn't take it any further. Pulling back, he glanced around the living room, expecting...what?

A comforting hand landed on his lower back. "I'll tell Lynda you're here."

Bo nodded and watched Jim head out of the room. He turned to Neil. "How's it been, having a baby in the house?"

Neil grinned. "I've actually enjoyed it. I wasn't around to watch Meadowlark grow up, so it's all pretty new for me."

Bo took the offered seat on the couch. "I don't know how to take care of a baby."

"No one really does until they're in the situation. It's a lot of gut feelings and even more patience. But the rewards are indescribable."

Bo could tell by the ex-Colonel's goofy grin he was telling the truth. Maybe Neil was right. He heard footsteps coming down the hall and turned to see Lynda holding a sleeping infant in her arms.

Rooted to the spot, Bo could do nothing but hold his breath and stare as she brought Joey closer.

"Would you like to hold him?" she asked.

Bo gazed down at the sleeping baby. "Isn't he a little small?"

Lynda smiled and ran her finger over Joey's cheek. "A little maybe, but not much."

She glanced up from the sweet child. "He's healthy, Bo."

Bo felt some of the tension slide from his shoulders. He eventually sat back down on the sofa and held out his arms. Lynda smiled and carefully handed the baby over. Joey's long black eyelashes fluttered before he drifted back to sleep. Despite the hair colour, it was easy to see Bo wasn't the father. The baby's dark bronze complexion was a sure sign.

Now that Joey was in his arms, Bo couldn't take his eyes off of him. So perfect. He grinned as Joey started dreaming, those red plump lips pursed and sucking an imaginary bottle.

His eyes began to burn with unshed tears. He didn't deserve something so innocent and clean. Shaking his head, he tried to hand Joey back to Lynda. "I can't."

"Yes, you can. We're going for lunch. You're in charge of Joey until we get back."

Before Bo could voice opposition, Lynda, Neil and Jim filed out the front door. He was left holding an infant he didn't know how to care for. Seeing no other choice, Bo sat back against the corner of the couch and propped his arm on one of the throw pillows.

"Looks like it's just you and me for an hour or so."

Twenty minutes after the threesome left, Joey woke. It started with a few grunts and fluttered eye movements. Bo tensed, not knowing what to expect. Those big black eyes opened and stared right at him.

The two of them studied each other for about five minutes before the crying started. Bo transferred Joey to his shoulder and tried to soothe the child that way, but it wasn't working. *Shit. Food, maybe he's hungry.*

Bo wasn't so clueless he didn't know to look for a bottle. He stood with Joey securely against his chest and went into the kitchen. The bottles were easy enough to find along with the formula, but the big question was how did he make one while holding a screaming, wiggling baby?

He knew setting Joey on the table or counter wasn't an option, so he dug out a couple of dishtowels and carefully laid Joey on top of them.

Reading the instructions on the can of formula, he worked as quickly as he could. "I'm trying, Joey. Give your old man a break."

He stopped mid-shake realising what he'd just said. *Well fuck.*

Bo finished the bottle and carried Joey out to the porch glider. He couldn't help but chuckle at the way the boy seemed to attack the bottle. "Damn, I guess you were hungry."

Berating himself for cussing in front of the boy, he made a mental note to clean up his language. As he watched Joey drain the bottle, he thought about Jan. He knew he needed to go see her, but there were a few things he needed to work out for himself first. It wouldn't do Jan's condition any good if he went in pissed.

A list. He needed to make a list of everything he'd need to do if he took Joey back to Cattle Valley with him. Of course there was the issue of where they'd live, but there was also childcare to think about as well as a host of other things. He knew one thing, he wouldn't feel right taking Joey until his mother had passed. What if she wanted to see her son's beautiful face once more before she took her last breath?

Joey finished the bottle and Bo lifted him to his shoulder like he'd seen mom's do on TV. He began patting the boy's back until he heard a belch and what sounded and felt like a good amount of upchuck. *Great.*

* * * *

Rance spotted Lark heading for his hybrid. Jogging after him, he called out. "Heard from Bo?"

Lark turned, wiping his sweaty face on the bottom of his T-shirt. "Yeah, he'll be home next week. Why?"

Rance kicked at the dirt under his boots. "Just wondering."

Lark cocked his hip to lean against the SUV. "Can I ask you something?"

Rance was afraid where this might go. "Maybe."

Taking several steps, Lark stared up into Rance's face. "Do you feel anything for him?"

Though he was expecting the question, it still set him off kilter. "He's a good guy, I guess. Good worker."

"That's not what I mean, and you know it."

Gazing down into the face of Bo's best friend, he knew he needed to try and explain what he couldn't seem to get across to Bo. "It doesn't matter whether I feel anything for him or not. I can't let it go anywhere, so he'd be better off setting his sights on someone else."

Lark nodded. "Normally I'd agree with you, but for whatever reason, he's fallen in love for the first time in his life. With everything else he's trying to deal with right now, he needs you."

Rance decided against addressing the love comment. "I thought he was getting better?"

"He is." Lark sighed and looked down at the ground. "He might kill me if he knew I told you this, but his wife died yesterday of heart failure."

Rance spun around, feeling like he'd been punched in the stomach. "He's married? Are you fucking kidding me?"

Oh, God, he was afraid he'd throw up. "That sonofabitch," he spat.

Rance stormed off towards his house, with Lark chasing after him.

"Wait. It's not what you think. He served Jan divorce papers over a year ago," Lark tried to explain.

"Save it, kid. You just told me everything I needed to know." He took the steps two at a time and shut the door in Lark's still protesting face.

* * * *

"You're sure you don't mind keeping Joey until I can get things set up back home?" Bo asked, bouncing Joey in his arms.

After their initial meeting, Bo had learned a lot about caring for the little guy. It helped that both Lynda and Joey were so patient with him. He looked at his son and grinned. "Are you daddy's boy?"

It no longer mattered to Bo that he wasn't Joey's biological father. The sweet baby had imbedded himself deep into Bo's heart. For the first time in his life he loved someone who seemed to love him back. He knew it was going to kill him to get on the plane back to Cattle Valley, but his time was up and he had a job he needed to return to.

"Daddy will be back to get you before you know it."

With one last kiss, Bo handed Joey over to Lynda. "I can't thank you enough for everything you've done for us."

Lynda leaned in and gave Bo a kiss on the cheek. "It's been my pleasure. And you know you're welcome anytime."

He gave a quick kiss goodbye to Jim and Neil, before smoothing his hand over the top of Joey's black hair. "I'll miss you."

Climbing into his rental car, he watched his son in the rear view mirror until he was a spec in the distance. Turning his eyes to the road, Bo concentrated on everything he needed to do to bring his son home.

Talking to Shep would be first on his list. He doubted his boss would mind if he lived off the ranch, but there was more to it than that. He'd need to make sure Shep understood that occasionally he'd need to leave work to take Joey to the doctor or whatever. His present plans were to try and keep Joey with him as much as possible during the day.

The women at Sunrise Gardens always toted their babies around with them in a pack on their back. Bo didn't see any reason why he couldn't do the same thing. He never messed with the livestock, and except for the incident with Zero breaking through the pen, he doubted he'd be putting Joey in any danger.

For days he'd worried about telling Rance, but then he'd looked into Joey's dark eyes and realised he couldn't expend time and energy loving someone who didn't want to be loved. He may never get over his feelings for Rance, but he couldn't afford to let them hold him back from living his life.

He dug the picture of Joey out of his front shirt pocket and kissed it. "Looks like it may just be you and me, kiddo."

Chapter Four

It wasn't until his second day back that Bo gathered the courage to speak to Shep. Knocking on the main house door, he took his customary seat on the porch swing and waited for Shep to join him.

It felt good to get his hands dirty again. He'd hated to put Lark out of a job, but he knew the boy was meant for better things anyway.

Shep stepped outside with Jeremy on his arm. "It's about time you came by."

"Sorry. I got in pretty late and I was eager to get started this morning."

"Lark told us about your wife. I'm sorry."

Bo nodded. It was still hard to imagine Jan was gone, but from the sound of it, she was in a better place. "I appreciate that. I guess she was in a lot of pain there towards the end. Did Lark happen to tell you anything else?"

Shep glanced at Jeremy, they both shook their heads. "Nope," Shep answered.

"Jan had a baby going on seven months ago. She left him for me to raise. And before ya ask, no, he's not mine by blood, but that don't make a spit of difference to me. I love Joey like he was my own."

Shep's eyes lit up and Jeremy's jaw dropped. "Hot damn. We're gonna have us a little mascot running around the ranch."

Jeremy elbowed Shep. "He's a baby, not a puppy."

Shep looked insulted. "I know that." He grinned at Bo. "I'm happy for you. I'm even happier for myself. I've always wanted a nephew to spoil."

Bo couldn't believe his boss was taking it so well. "Just so you know. I'll be looking for a house for the two of us in town. I hope that's okay."

"No. It certainly is not okay. What's wrong with the bunkhouse? Now that Jeremy's not sharing your room there should be plenty of space for a crib."

Bo scratched his head. "I'm not so sure the other cowboys will be as excited about Joey as you are."

"Well, why don't you ask 'em before you run out and buy a house? It should work for a couple years at least."

He'd never get over the kindness of the folks in Cattle Valley. Bo went on to tell Shep and Jeremy all about the baby, even bringing out the few pictures he'd brought along. By the end of their visit, he reckoned Jeremy was almost as taken with the idea of having a baby around as Shep.

"It's Tuesday, which means Taco Night in town. Care to join us?"

Bo rubbed his stomach. It had been over two months since he'd sat down to eat greasy tacos with his friends. "I'd love to. Sunrise Garden's is great if you want fresh produce, but it sucks if you're hankering for junk food. Just let me run to the house and get cleaned up, ten minutes max."

Shep nodded. "We'll be here."

Bo jogged towards the bunkhouse. Flying through the door, he almost ran over Rance. "Sorry," he said and kept going.

Stripping off his clothes, he jumped into a warm shower, and quickly scrubbed up. For the first time in recent memory, the sight of Rance hadn't made him hard. Bo thought that was pretty good progress.

He was out of the shower and dressed in comfortable shorts and a white muscle shirt within eight minutes, leaving two to spare. After slipping on his flip-flops, he ran a brush through his hair and was out the door.

"Made it," he panted, running up the porch steps.

It was then he noticed Shep and Jeremy enjoying an evening make-out session. Damn. I guess there had been no need for him to rush after all. One thing the cowboys on the ranch had learned pretty damn quick, was not to interrupt the boss when he was gettin' some sugar.

Resigned to waiting, he climbed back down the steps and took a seat. He was surprised when Rance's big black truck pulled up in front of him.

"Need a ride? Looks like they may be awhile."

Bo didn't even need to look over his shoulder. The slurping kissing and moaning sounds were enough to let him know Rance was right. With a deep breath and a renewed pledge to himself, Bo climbed into the truck. "Thanks, I appreciate it."

As they drove towards town, the only words Rance said to him had to do with work. "The hay should be about ready, won't it?"

"Yeah. I'll probably start cuttin' and bailing next week. I'm gonna need some help loading the small bales though. The doc released me to come back to work, but I've got a weight restriction of thirty pounds until he clears me."

"No problem."

They rode the rest of the way in complete silence. Bo eventually reached over and turned the radio on low. He couldn't help but to wonder if things between him and Rance would always be strained.

One thing he knew for sure was he needed to tell Rance about Joey. Bo decided to wait until the ride home for that. No sense ruining both their dinners, because there was no doubt they'd probably fight about it. That just seemed to be Rance's way lately.

Bo wasn't even surprised when Rance chose to sit at the opposite end of the long table reserved for the cowhands from EZ Does It and Back Breaker. They'd all been eating together for years he'd heard.

He ordered a pitcher of beer, earning a dirty look from Rance. *Fuck you.* By the time he'd finished his first glass, Jax, Logan, Kade and Lark strolled through the door. Finally, someone for him to talk to.

Lark greeted Bo with a big hug. "I've missed you."

"I missed you, too. How's the job hunt?"

Lark chuckled and rolled his eyes. "I've only been out of a job for one day. I think I deserve at least a couple weeks off before I become a full-fledged adult."

Bo reached over and mussed Lark's blond hair. "I reckon you're right."

Lark practically bounced in his chair. "So tell me about Joey. I want to hear everything."

Bo leaned back and crossed his arms. Now this was a topic he'd gladly talk about. "He's beautiful. I swear I've never seen anyone more perfect. He's got jet black hair and the prettiest bronze skin you ever laid eyes on. Oh, speaking of eyes. His will absolutely mesmerise you, long thick lashes that kind of fan over his cheeks when he blinks. I tell ya, Lark, I knew I was in love the first time I held him in my arms."

A disturbance at the other end of the table caught his attention. Rance had up-ended the beer he'd been drinking and it was spilling all over Ezra.

"Oh, shit," Bo chuckled. Spilling beer on a man the size of Ezra James was like poking a stick at a grizzly.

He winked at Lark. "If Ezra decides to kill Rance, will you give me a lift home?"

* * * *

After apologising profusely to Ezra, Rance decided he'd had enough beer. His gaze slid to Bo at the opposite end of the table. The man was drinking like a fish. Didn't he understand how bad beer was for him?

Hell, he was probably too busy pining for that guy, Joey, he'd been talking about earlier. Rance didn't know if Bo had done it on purpose, but the man was talking loud enough for Rance to hear every word.

Maybe he should be happy Bo had found someone while in Canada, but dammit, it proved to him once again that he was easily forgotten. Bo was the second person to claim he was in love with him, only to brush him aside when something better came along. Well, fine. It would definitely make his life easier. He'd been really starting to rethink things when Bo had stayed away for so long.

"You ready?" Bo asked.

Rance looked up and was surprised most of the people at the table had already paid their bills and left. "Yeah."

Throwing a couple bills onto the table, he walked out to his truck. He regretted ever offering Bo a ride in the first place. But, just as he'd suspected, Shep and Jeremy never actually made it into O'Brien's for Taco Tuesday.

* * * *

"Don't puke in my truck," Rance growled as he fastened his seat belt.

"What? Why would I puke? I only had three beers."

"Three too many as far as I'm concerned," Rance grumbled.

"What's your problem, man?" Bo asked.

"It's not good for you, and you know it. I thought you were supposed to be some kind of expert at taking care of yourself."

Bo's eyes slid to study Rance's profile. It almost sounded like the man was concerned. Bo tried to push the idea away, but he wondered the rest of the drive home.

Once they pulled up in the ranch yard, Bo realised he hadn't told Rance about Joey. Oh well, he didn't seem in the mood anyway. Maybe he'd catch him in the morning. Of course that meant he should hold off talking to Steve, Buddy and Jim.

Bo got out of the truck and headed for the bunkhouse. He wondered if it was too late to call Lynda and check on Joey? *Oh crap.* That reminded him. He'd left his cell phone on the tractor.

Veering off from his original destination, Bo walked towards the pasture. The tractor was beyond the second gate, and he'd have to cross the bull pen, but it was late and usually the big guys were calm at night.

He heard footsteps behind him and glanced over his shoulder. Rance was closing in. What the hell did he want?

"Where do you think you're going?" Rance asked.

Bo never broke stride. He climbed over the first gate, but made the mistake of jumping down. A stitch of pain had him reaching for his previous injury.

"I asked you a question."

Bo exhaled. He'd been trying to get through the pen as quiet as possible which wasn't going to happen if Rance kept up the interrogation. "I left my phone in the tractor, so I'm going to get it, is that okay with you?"

He was almost to the second gate when Rance put a hand on his shoulder. "You're a damn fool, you know that?"

Bo shrugged the hand off and unlocked the gate. After the first idiot move, he didn't plan on making another. He slipped in through the open fence and went to close it, but once again Rance was there.

Bo tried his best to keep his cool, but Rance just kept on. "What the hell you need your phone bad enough for that you'd risk your neck walking through a pen of bulls?"

Spinning to face Rance, Bo pushed him. "What the fuck is your problem? For a year you act like you can't stand to be around me, now all of a sudden you're my keeper. Bullshit! I want to call and see if Joey's still awake. Is that okay with you, Boss?"

Rance started chuckling. "Oh, I should've guessed. One day away from your new fuck buddy and you'd…"

That's as far as Rance got before Bo ploughed his fist into his boss's pretty face. Caught off guard, Rance landed on the ground. Before he could get up, Bo towered over him, pointing a finger directly in Rance's face.

"You ever say something like that about my son again and I'll kill ya."

Rance looked surprised. He rubbed his jaw where Bo's fist had connected. "Joey's your son? Since when do you have a kid?"

"Yeah he's my son, who the hell did you think he was?" Bo was surprised Rance even knew Joey's name.

"Hell, I didn't know. I heard you telling Lark at dinner how gorgeous he was and how you were so in love with him. What was I supposed to think?"

Before Bo could explain any further, a noise behind them caught his attention.

"Fuck! Run!" he screamed, taking off towards the tractor as Zero Tolerance charged through the open gate and straight for them.

Both barely managed to jump on the tractor before the one ton bull reached them. "Why didn't you shut the goddamn gate?"

"I thought I did," Rance yelled back.

Without getting down, Bo climbed from the back tire to the cab. He held out his hand to Rance. "Best come on over here. Doesn't look like old Zero's going anywhere, anytime soon."

After a several second staring contest between the two men, Rance eventually let Bo help him to the open cab. Zero continued to snot and snort his way around the tractor. Bo could tell the mean sonofabitch was just waiting for his chance to get them.

Bo retrieved his cell phone from under the seat. "Should we call somebody?"

Rance chuckled. "Seriously? Do you know how bad we'll get dogged for this?"

Although the cab was bigger than the width of the tire, it was still too small for two people to stand or sit for the hours it may take for Zero to get tired of the game.

"Go ahead and take a seat. I'll climb up on the hood."

"No, you take the seat. You're the one who's still on the mend."

Bo wasn't about to get into a pissing contest with Rance over who sat where, so he took the offered seat. "Thanks."

Rance climbed over the steering wheel and straddled the hood as much as he could while still keeping his legs higher than Zero could reach. The two of them sat in silence for about fifteen minutes before Rance finally cleared his throat.

"So tell me about your boy."

"Well, I guess there's no time like the present." Bo went on to explain to Rance about Jan, her pregnancy and subsequent illness. He waxed poetic about his son and how smart he was.

"You've tested his IQ already?" Rance chuckled.

"Of course not. You can tell by the way he looks at you though that he's thinking of all kinds of things. I wouldn't be surprised if he started talking any day.

Rance laughed again. "Been around a lot of talking babies, have ya?"

"Never been around babies, period. Joey's the first, so cut me some slack."

"I'll think about it. So when are you bringing him down here?"

"Soon. I need to talk to the guys and make sure they don't mind a baby in the bunkhouse. I offered to buy a place in town, but Shep wouldn't hear of it. I think he's looking forward to playing uncle."

"I can't wait to see that."

They'd been so involved they hadn't even noticed Zero had gone. "Shit. Where'd he go?"

"I don't know," Rance said. "But I doubt he went back in the pen."

"What're we gonna do?" Bo asked. All he could think about was Shep hitting the roof when he found out his number one rodeo bull was AWOL.

"I guess we get up in the morning and go find him. Might take more than a day depending on how motivated he is to get the fuck outa Dodge."

Bo groaned. "Perfect. I guess there's no way around telling Shep now, is there?"

"It's my fault. I'll tell Shep I left the gate open."

"I can't let you take the fall by yourself. We'll go to him together at first light."

Rance looked around once more. "You ready to make a break for it?"

"Might as well. I'm sure if the big bastard is anywhere in the area, he'll come running. I still don't know why he hates me so much."

Rance chuckled as he slid to the ground. "Don't take it personally. Zero hates everyone."

"Some it seems more than others."

* * * *

Rance didn't dare look at Bo. Shep had given them both an ass-chewin' they'd not soon forget. He'd ordered them out with the stock trailer, telling them not to come back without the bull.

"At least we don't have to worry about Zero going up into the high country," he mumbled. Bulls as big and heavy as Zero tended to take the easiest route to reach a destination.

"There is that," Bo agreed.

They could also be thankful they had the pickup, and not the horses. Riding for days on horseback wasn't as fun as it sounded. He still couldn't believe he'd left the damn gate open. What a sophomoric thing to do. If he'd been paying more attention to the livestock, instead of his jealous streak, he'd have never made the mistake.

There, he'd admitted it. He'd been jealous when he'd overheard Bo talking about Joey. The really stupid part was that even after finding out that Joey was a baby, he was still jealous. Evidently he'd gotten so used to Bo always there, trying to kiss him, or brushing a hand over Rance's butt when he passed by, there seemed to be a void without it.

Bo must be a hell of a guy to agree to raise another man's child. That's what got him most of all. Now that he knew the truth, he was questioning everything he'd ever thought about Bo. He'd heard Bo talking about the sex-commune or whatever they called it on many occasions, and from that he'd formed an opinion about the man that was turning out to be very wrong.

"How long were you married?" he found himself asking.

"Three years legal. Two years together."

"Did you love her?"

Bo shifted in the seat to lean against the passenger door. "I cared for her. But love, no, I can't say that I did."

"This may be a dumb question, but why'd you marry her if you didn't love her?"

Bo didn't answer for several moments. Finally, he cleared his throat. "I guess I just wanted to belong to somebody."

The pain in the simple answer tore at Rance's heart. "What about family?"

Bo shrugged. "My friends are my family. I ran away from home, if you could even call it that, when I was thirteen."

"Damn. You were just a kid."

"Yeah."

"How'd you survive?"

Bo readjusted himself and rolled down the window. "Any way I could."

Rance knew by the way he'd said it that Bo had traded his body for survival. "Is that how you contracted the virus?"

"You're awfully nosy for someone who won't tell me a flying fig about his own past."

"You're right. I'm sorry for buttin' in."

They drove miles trying to cover every inch of the east pasture before finding a broken spot in the fencing. "Shit."

Rance parked the truck and got out to inspect the fence. A tuft of black hair stuck to one of the barbs on the broken wire. "Well at least he made it through and didn't kill himself."

"Yeah, but where does this go?"

Rance sighed. "Beauregard Game Preserve."

"Shit."

"Yep."

* * * *

After spending over an hour on the phone with Shep and Nate, Rance was finally given the go ahead to take the truck and trailer onto the game preserve's land. The only stipulation was he needed to put a temporary fix on the fence after Bo drove through with the trailer.

Without proper tools, and protective gloves, the danger of Bo cutting himself was too great for them to take the chance. Rance did his best to rig a solution out of the already stretched and broken wire.

By the time he hopped into the truck, another ninety minutes had passed. "Cross your fingers that thing holds until I can get back to the ranch."

"Where to?" Bo asked.

Rance looked over at Bo. He knew the guy felt bad about not being able to help with the fence, but they didn't have any other option. "Go ahead and head straight east. Zero's not the smartest bull in the pen, so I doubt he's trying to trick us."

Bo nodded and slowly drove the pickup and trailer over the rocks and brush. "Yeah," Bo said out of the blue.

"Huh?"

"When I was seventeen, a man named Edward made me his boy toy. I travelled the world, wore expensive clothes and contracted the virus, while sailing the Mediterranean. You see, there was a rare vintage of wine Edward had his eye on, but the only thing the owner would take in exchange was a night with me."

Bo slowed the truck to a stop and leaned his head against the steering wheel. "The bastard knew he had the virus, that's why he made the deal. Edward wouldn't sleep with him, so he infected Edward through me."

Rance closed his eyes and put a hand on Bo's back. "I'm sorry."

Bo wiped his eyes and turned his head to look at Rance. "Ya know, I've done a lot of things in my life and I've met some very interesting people. One thing that I've learned is that everyone has a story, and everyone thinks theirs is the worst."

Bo chuckled. "That's why I don't dwell on mine. It sucks that I've lived over thirteen years with a virus that makes a lot of people fear me, but I can't change it. All I can do is wake up each morning, and thank God I was granted another day."

Rance had to turn away from the honesty in Bo's eyes. Was it shame he was feeling? Had he shut himself off from people and intimacy for sixteen years because he simply felt sorry for himself?

Bo started the truck and continued driving east as Rance attempted to keep his focus on the task at hand. He knew he had a lot to think about. Who would've thought the guy who joked with everyone, would be the one to make him see the truth behind his actions?

* * * *

Because they weren't allowed to build a fire on the preserve's land, Rance decided it would be best to sleep in the stock trailer, at least it would afford them protection from the animals.

As Bo disrobed to his underwear and crawled inside his sleeping bag, he couldn't get the afternoon's morose conversation out of his mind. Why had he spilled his guts to a man who didn't seem to care? The answer came to Bo almost immediately, *because Rance does care*. Bo had seen it in Rance's eyes when he'd finished his story.

Rance being tight-lipped the rest of the day threw him a bit, but he knew it wasn't anger driving the silence. He wondered if Rance was looking for an opening. It was harder for men to admit they'd made a mistake, Bo knew that as well as anyone.

"Can I ask you something?"

"Maybe." Rance replied, cautiously.

"There are two stories about you floating around Cattle Valley and I'd sure as hell like to know which one is correct. Were you on the pro rodeo circuit before you moved here, or did you come from Boston?"

He'd purposely asked that question because he already knew the answer. Everyone in town thought Rance was a rodeo retiree, but only a few knew Rance's true history. Bo needed to test Rance for whatever reason to see if he'd open up and tell him the truth.

"Never rode in a real rodeo in my life. I spent summers with my grandparents in Oklahoma. There wasn't much else for a kid to do there besides learn to ride. After summer break, I'd return to my parent's upscale brownstone in Boston."

Bo felt like pumping his arms into the air at the small victory. He rolled to his side and readjusted the inflatable pillow under his head. "Never been to Oklahoma. Weird since I grew up in Missouri. Guess there was just never a reason to go there."

Rance turned to face Bo and grinned. "You didn't miss much."

"So why'd you go?"

"Probably the same reason you got married. My parents were very busy people with important and time consuming careers. I went to Oklahoma to get treated like I mattered."

Bo reached out and cupped the side of Rance's face. Leaning further in, he whispered against Rance's lips. "I think the two of us have more in common than we want to admit."

Rance closed the distance and sealed his lips with Bo's. The kiss started soft, with playful nips thrown in for fun.

Bo moaned and scooted his bed closer to Rance. He felt like a butterfly trapped in a cocoon. Laying half on top of Rance, Bo took the kiss deeper, tasting, sucking. Kissing Rance was everything good in the world rolled into one package.

With his cock stone hard, Bo's body automatically started grinding against Rance. At first Rance seemed to welcome the increased sexual activity, but just like previously, he panicked and called a halt to it.

"Stop. Bo, please, stop," he cried, pushing Bo away.

Bo rolled over on his back and flung his arm over his eyes. "Jesus you're a hard guy to figure out."

With an audible sigh, Rance moved over and put his head on Bo's chest. "You know how you said earlier that everyone has a story? Well I have one too, and I think it's finally time I shared it with you."

Chapter Five

Bo wrapped his arm around Rance. It hadn't escaped him that the man didn't take off anything but his hat and boots before climbing into his sleeping bag. As he tried to put Rance at ease by running a comforting hand up and down his arm, the feel of material was out of place.

"Before you start, will you do me a favour and at least take your shirt off? Snuggling's much better skin to skin."

"Ummm, maybe you should hear my story first."

Bo kissed the top of Rance's head. "Doesn't matter what kind of story you tell me, I'll still want your shirt off."

Rance's muscles tensed under Bo's hands. The more Bo thought about it, the more he realised he'd never seen Rance without a shirt. Even on the hottest days of the year, the furthest Rance went was a muscle shirt.

Leaning back, Rance sat up and pulled his T-shirt over his head and laid it to the side. With only the moonlight streaming in through the top of the stock trailer, Bo couldn't make out anything unusual about Rance's chest. As he'd expect of a hard working man like Rance, the muscles were sculpted. Other than being pale in contrast to the cowboys face, neck and arms, Rance's chest looked as perfect as Bo knew it would.

With a deep breath, Rance reached down and brought Bo's hand to his lower stomach. "Feel this?"

Bo's fingers encountered a mass of small scars pebbled across Rance's stomach. "Can I ask?"

"Let me give you the Reader's Digest version."

"Okay," Bo agreed, pulling Rance back down into his arms.

"I started dating this guy, Oren, when I worked for the Boston PD. With my crazy schedule, we didn't see a lot of each other, but we tried to make time for a couple dates a week. I always thought it was strange that he'd refused to stay the night, but his excuses were always believable."

"Oh, shit," Bo mumbled. He had a feeling he knew where this was going.

"Yeah, oh, shit. About seven months into the relationship, a woman walked up to me as I was getting off-shift. It was raining, so I didn't think anything by the long trench coat she was wearing. She asked me if I was Rance Benning."

Bo swallowed around the lump in his throat. He didn't like the direction this story was heading. He held Rance closer.

"When I said yes, she pulled out a shotgun loaded with a round of buckshot and fired, almost point blank. She aimed for my dick, but like buckshot's known to do, the spray covered a pretty large area."

Bo gasped as his balls immediately tried to hide inside his body. So many things came back to him at that point, like the kiss in Rance's office. They'd been going at it hot and heavy until Bo had reached for Rance's erection.

Bo tried to speak, but found he couldn't. He cleared his throat and tried again. "What happened?"

"My fellow officers heard the shot and came pouring out of the building. Oren's *wife*, Anita, didn't even try to run. They called an ambulance and managed to get me to the hospital before I bled to death. I ended up having four separate procedures to try and reconstruct the damage that one shotgun blast caused. They did everything they could, but my body was too badly damaged. I lost a nut, and my cock was basically split in two. They sewed me back together. Even after all these years I can't stand to look at myself."

"What happened to Oren and his wife?"

"Anita stood trial. She's still in prison, will be for another few years. Oren, now that's the saddest part of all. After the shooting, an ex-lover of his came forward. The guy told the police that Oren's wife had caught the two of them in bed. She told Oren the next time he decided to fuck around, she'd blow the balls off the guy. Needless to say, the guy he was having a fling with took to the hills."

"So he knew he was putting you in danger?"

"Yeah, and the prosecutor and I thought he did it on purpose. You see, Anita was a wealthy woman. Oren knew he'd get shafted if he tried to divorce her. The next best thing was sending her to prison. And who better to have your wife shoot than a cop. Yeah, Oren knew exactly what he was doing."

"So is he in jail, too?"

"No. In the end, the prosecutor didn't feel she had enough proof to take the case to trial."

"He's a free man?"

"Yep. Something I think about every time I use the john."

Bo finally understood. Not only was Rance betrayed in the worst way, but he was left with a constant reminder. The size and shape of a man's penis was a huge part of his self-esteem. No wonder Rance refused to let anyone get close to him.

Pulling Rance up until he was eye level, Bo kissed him. Keeping his lips gentle, he tried to convey the depths of his sorrow for what Rance had gone through. It must have worked, because Rance's body began to shake as his emotions got the better of him.

Bo broke the kiss and Rance laid his head on Bo's outstretched arm. Gazing into each other's eyes, Bo brushed his lips over Rance's forehead. "If this right here is the most you're ever able to give, I'll be content for the rest of my life. My love for you has nothing to do with sex, which I know sounds strange coming from a guy like me, but it's the truth. Just to feel you in my arms every night will be more than I've ever hoped for."

Rance began peppering kisses on Bo's naked chest. "Hmmm, that doesn't sound like much fun. The equipment still works. It's just not something I'm comfortable with you seeing, at least not yet anyway."

"I can live with that. I guess this is the part of the conversation where we should talk about my positive status, huh?"

Rance ducked his head, rimming his tongue around Bo's pebbled nipple before answering. "I already know quite a bit. To be perfectly honest, shortly after you came to Cattle Valley I looked HIV up on the internet. So the way I see it, as long as we lay in a large supply of condoms, I think we should be okay in that respect. Although you know I'll probably continue to nag you about your diet."

Bo laughed for the first time in what felt like days. "I'm actually a very healthy eater. Sure I like to indulge from time to time, but I know what my body needs to remain in good shape."

Rance ran his hand over Bo's chest. "Yeah, you must, because no one looking at you would even know you're positive."

"And that's the way I intend to keep it."

Joey's face popped into his head. *Shit.* They hadn't even discussed his son. "Can I ask you a question?"

Rance chuckled. "I think it's safe to say I'm pretty much an open book to you at this point."

"Well…damn, I feel like a girl."

Rance's hand brushed over the erection trapped in Bo's underwear. "Hmm, you don't feel like one."

"Smart ass. The thing is, I have my son to think about now. And I guess…I just need to know if you see this thing between us lasting."

Rance leaned up on his elbow and looked down at Bo. "Do you have any idea what it meant for me to tell you that story?"

Before Bo could answer, Rance leaned down and kissed him. "I love you, you stupid ass."

Bo grinned from ear to ear. "What about Joey? Is there room in your life for him?"

"I've not been around many babies. Delivered one once, but that's the extent of my knowledge."

"Hell, you know more than I did when I went to Canada. Lynda, that's Lark's mom, she taught me quite a bit. I could teach you if you want me to."

Rolling over on top of Bo, Rance began to grind their hips together. "And what sort of treat will I get if I pass a lesson?"

Bo's hands squeezed between them, and went to the snaps on Rance's jeans. "Is this okay?"

After a short pause, Rance nodded. "I'll get them."

He rolled off Bo and began to strip. Bo took off his own underwear and waited for Rance to finish. It didn't escape his notice that Rance turned the slightest bit away from Bo when he pulled his underwear off.

Reaching for his jeans, Bo dug out his wallet and withdrew two condom packets. Before Rance could question Bo's reason for carrying them, Bo decided to put his soon-to-be lover's mind at ease. "When I found out I was positive, I vowed to never leave home without a supply. Don't worry though. I've not needed them since moving to Cattle Valley, at least not until now."

Kneeling on his sleeping bag, Rance used his T-shirt to cover himself while he began unzipping the bag. "Why don't we put our bags together?"

Although he doubted they'd need any covers, Bo nodded and rose off his makeshift mattress. He grinned several times as he caught Rance's gaze zeroing in on his bouncing cock.

"All for you," he teased, waving his erection from side to side with a shake of his hips.

Before he even had their bed made, Rance was busy tearing open one of the foil packets. "Is two all you have?"

Bo chuckled. "Yep. Sorry."

Rance scratched his jaw for a few seconds, apparently deep in thought. "My cum holds no danger to you, right?"

"Yeah, but I won't suck you off without a condom. Although the risk to you is minimal, it's just not worth it."

"Okay, so, if I suit you up, suck you off, and then rub off on you, we'd only use one condom, right?"

Bo's cock began producing copious amounts of pre-cum at the idea. "Yeah."

"Perfect. Then that would leave another one for morning."

Laughing, Bo thrust his cock towards Rance. "Sounds like a plan."

Rance held out the condom and slowly rolled it down Bo's length, giving the reservoir at the tip plenty of space for Bo's seed. "That enough room?"

Bo was so lost in the hand-job Rance was giving him, he found it hard to answer. "Good."

As he struggled to get into the sleeping bag, Rance refused to remove his hand from Bo's erection. Damn. Bo didn't know if he'd ever felt so much pleasure from a simple hand-job.

Unzipping the bag far enough to expose Bo's cock to the air, Rance leaned down. The first brush of Rance's tongue nearly sent Bo over the edge. "Fuck, babe."

"Goddamn you're big," Rance observed, teasing Bo's length with his tongue.

"All yours," he mumbled, as Rance's mouth covered the crown.

Bless Rance for not commenting on the nasty taste of the latex. Instead, he seemed to be enthralled with Bo's cock, taking as much of the length as he could into his throat. Bo knew it had been years for Rance, so he wasn't bothered the few times when his lover gagged.

"Don't hurt yourself. If you wanna suck the head, that's more than fine with me."

Rance refused his offer and continued to try and stretch his throat enough to take more of Bo's length. Bo couldn't help but grin. Rance was a man who needed to be the best at everything he did. And from the way he was making Bo feel, he didn't need to worry about his blow job abilities.

Once Rance seemed more comfortable, Bo let himself go, threading his fingers through Rance's dark hair as he began to fuck his lover's mouth. "Oh, Christ you're good at that."

With his balls tightening, Bo warned Rance of his impending climax. "Almost there."

Rance's fingers danced over Bo's scrotum and asshole as he continued the assault on Bo's cock. He sucked in his breath as the first pulse of cum shot from his shaft into the tight latex.

With his hand working the base, Rance continued to milk every drop of cum from Bo's cock. Reaching down, Bo pulled Rance up and into a deep kiss.

"That was...amazing." Bo gave Rance another kiss before carefully removing the condom. With no idea where to dispose of it, he dug, one handed into his duffle and removed the baggie he had his toothbrush in. Dropping the tied condom inside, he set it aside.

"Wow. You're really careful," Rance commented.

Bo removed one of the moist towellets he always carried in his duffle and thoroughly cleaned his cock. "I'm a bit obsessive actually, but I never want to do to a lover what was done to me. It's a small price to pay for peace of mind."

As soon as Bo had put the towellet into the baggie, Rance growled and rolled on top of him. "My turn."

"How do you want me?" Bo asked.

"Just as you are," Rance chuckled, starting a slow grind.

Bo had to be honest. He longed to reach down and hold his lover's shaft in his hand, but at this point in their relationship, he wasn't sure his touch would be welcomed. The truth was, he didn't want to hold Rance's cock out of some sense of morbid curiosity, he wanted to touch it because it was attached to the sexiest man he'd ever known.

The intensity in which Rance was grinding against him, Bo could very well imagine what making love with the ranch foreman would be like. For all his quiet reserve, Rance was surprising him at every turn.

With a hand to the back of Rance's neck, he pulled the sexy sonofabitch down into a deep, tongue fucking kiss.

A grunt, followed by an all-over body shiver signalled Rance's orgasm. "Oh, fuck."

Bo welcomed the heat of his lover's seed as it shot between their bodies. He pushed his hand between them, and gathered as much of Rance's essence as he could. Bringing his fingers to his lips, Bo stared into his partner's eyes as he slowly licked at the thick, white cum.

Rance groaned and leaned down for another kiss, sweeping his tongue into Bo's mouth to taste his own flavour.

"Mmmm," Bo hummed. "You taste good."

Rance reached into Bo's bag and extracted another towelett. After a quick clean-up, he collapsed on Bo's chest. "You've worn me out."

"And that was with just one condom. Imagine what we could do with an entire box at our disposal."

* * * *

During the early hours of the morning, the entire trailer tilted as a loud noise woke Rance and Bo from a sound sleep.

"What the hell?" Bo shot up onto his feet.

The trailer listed to its side, as once again it was rocked by what Rance suspected was a one ton fucker named Zero Tolerance.

Scrambling for his clothes, Rance began to turn in circles. "Where's my goddamn underwear."

"Forget 'em. We've got to get that sonofabitch in here before he gets away again. Bo threw on his clothes and started to climb the lumbar walls of the trailer.

Another hit threatened to send Bo toppling over the top. "What the hell are you doing?" Rance asked.

"Trying to get the hell out of here without getting myself killed. I thought if I could make it to the hitch, I could climb into the back of the truck."

"And then what? You gonna take on Zero by yourself?" Rance yelled.

"I guess unless you get your clothes on, I will."

It was then that Rance realised he was still standing in the centre of the trailer completely naked. "Shit."

He found his jeans and quickly stepped into them, hoping it was still too dark for Bo to have seen him.

"So how're we gonna play this?" he asked, pulling his T-shirt over his head.

"Uhhh, drop the back and chase him in with a couple of baseball bats?"

Rance rolled his eyes even though he knew the gesture went unseen. "How about we try the lassos first and then move to the bats as a back-up plan?"

"You love to ruin my fun. Have you forgotten what that beast did to me?"

Rance paused in the act of sliding on his boot and gazed up at Bo. "No. I'll never forget what happened to you. I've seen it enough in my dreams to have a permanent imprint on my brain."

Bo grinned down at him. The first rays of sun were slowly peaking up from the horizon, casting his lover in a soft orange glow. "I've got a box of condoms back at the ranch. What say you bring that sweet ass up here and help me wrangle this ornery bull."

Rance nodded and tossed Bo his duffle, slinging his own over his shoulder. "What about the sleeping bags?"

Zero hit the trailer with an echoing grunt. Rance began to climb the opposite wall. "Fuck the bags. Can ya get the bolt on that side while I release this one?"

Rance took hold of the bolt and waited for Bo. "On three. One, two, three!"

The bolts were pulled simultaneously, allowing the back gate to drop to the ground. Rance smiled and winked. "Now we just have to make it to the lassos in the truck bed."

"Or the baseball bat that I always keep behind the seat," Bo added.

Shaking his head, Rance jumped down and moved to the front of the trailer and once again climbed up the wooden slats. He was halfway up when he heard Bo lower himself to the trailer floor. Swinging his leg over the top rail, he turned back to Bo. Shit.

"Uh, Bo?"

"What?" Bo paused with his foot on the first board.

Rance pointed at Zero Tolerance who stood at the bottom of the ramp with murder in his eyes. "You might wanna hurry."

* * * *

"And then, Bo climbs that damn wall faster than Spider Man," Rance doubled over in laughter as the rest of the hands joined him.

Bo rolled his eyes and stared at Zero through the slit in the boards. "Isn't it bad enough you caused me to miss planting? Now you have to make me the butt of jokes among my lover and my friends? I'm soooo disappointed in you."

Zero's head butted the two by six in front of Bo's face hard enough to splinter it, catching the cowboys' attention. As the ranch hands scrambled to get the trailer backed up to Zero's pen, the animal started destroying everything in sight. Bits of Bo and Rance's sleeping bags floated in the air like plaid confetti.

Jim and Buddy climbed up the sides of the trailer to release the bolts. When the ramp came down, Zero stormed towards it, huffing and snorting up a storm. Bo had never seen or heard anything like it.

The ramp bowed under the bull's tremendous weight as he made his way into his pen. Bo's first look at the bull had him cracking up.

"Those must be yours," he hollered to Rance.

A red-faced Rance shook his head at the one ton bull parading around the pen with Rance's boxer briefs caught on one horn.

Another round of laughter ensued, surpassing the one earlier. Bo smiled, satisfied. His work was done.

Sliding up behind Rance, Bo whispered in his ear as he casually brushed his hand across his lover's ass. "I don't know about you, but I could sure use a shower."

Rance looked over his shoulder, worry in his eyes. "I can't. Tonight? Maybe we could go out or something?"

The insecure expression on Rance's face melted his heart. Despite the still cackling cowboys, Bo leaned in and placed a soft kiss on Rance's neck. "You've got yourself a date."

As he walked towards the bunkhouse, Bo took a calming breath. "I'm gonna break down that final wall if it's the last thing I do."

Chapter Six

Bo knocked on Rance's door at seven o'clock sharp. He dressed in his fanciest duds, which wasn't saying a whole lot. Still, he thought he looked presentable in his dark jeans, white dress shirt and black leather vest.

Rance opened the door and Bo almost fell to his knees.

"Goddamn you're hot." No matter what Bo did, he'd never be able to compete with Rance in the looks department. The man was fine with a capital F. Dressed all in black, with a big silver belt buckle, Rance's clothes definitely drew attention to the large bulge behind the man's fly. Scarred or not, that dick was something to be proud of.

After settling his black dress Stetson onto his head, Rance leaned in for a kiss. "You look pretty damn good yourself."

Bo moved even closer, wrapping his arms around his lover. Groin to groin, Bo did a slow slide. "We could always stay in?"

Rance nodded. "Yeah, we could, but I'd kinda like to do a little courtin' before we jump into bed. Besides, if people see us out and about together maybe it'll put some of the rumours of me being straight to rest."

Chuckling, Bo kissed Rance again, this time pushing his tongue in to taste the minty-flavoured toothpaste Rance had obviously just used. "Cattle Valley is a little backward compared to most towns, but I never believed for a second that you were a straight man hiding out in town."

"Erico's the one who started the whole damn thing."

"Why, doesn't he like you?" Bo asked.

"At one time he liked me a little too much and couldn't figure out why he couldn't get into my pants. He figured I must be straight to turn him down."

Bo placed soft kisses down Rance's jaw. "His loss."

"If we don't get out of here, our first official date will be ruined."

Before releasing the man in his arms, Bo pressed his face to Rance's neck and inhaled. The smell was fantastic. Rance mixed with something soft and citrus. "You've never worn cologne for me before."

"Don't wear it much, draws mosquitoes," Rance explained in a matter of fact tone.

Bo rolled his eyes and pulled his date out the front door. What a romantic he had on his hands.

Rance opened the driver's side door and Bo climbed in, sitting in the middle. Once they were both buckled up, Bo captured Rance's lips in yet another kiss. "You're addictive."

"Good. I'm glad you feel that way." Rance slung his arm across the back of the seat and backed out.

"So, where're we going?" Bo asked.

"Well I thought you might enjoy a nice steak dinner at the Grizzly Bar. Maybe even take a turn or two around the dance floor while we're there."

"Sounds good. I've only been there once, and then only for drinks."

Rance's hand started playing with Bo's hair as they made the drive up the mountain. "So when're you bringing Joey down?"

The question surprised Bo. "Why? Are you looking forward to meeting him?"

"Well sure. I mean, I never thought it would be possible to have a kid, but since I've been thinking about it, I'm getting pretty damn excited by the whole idea."

The statement made Bo feel all gooey and sappy, something he definitely wouldn't divulge to the rough and tumble cowboy next to him. "I'm happy you feel that way because Jim, Lynda and Neil are bringing him down on the private plane on Saturday. I offered to come back up, but they said they wanted to see Lark and Kade anyway. They've also been gracious enough to give me all the baby stuff they bought for Joey."

Rance removed his arm from the back of the seat when the roads began to wind their way up the mountain. Bo could tell by the expression on Rance's face he was deep in thought.

"Something wrong?" Bo asked.

"Huh? No, I was just thinking."

"About?"

"Nothing in particular." Rance reached down and squeezed Bo's thigh. "It's a lot to take in. You'll need to be patient with me."

Bo nodded. "I know. I'm trying."

He let the subject drop, but it continued to bother him. They reached the lodge and went inside. Walking into the Grizzly Bar was like old home week.

"What the hell are all these people doing here on a weeknight?" Rance asked.

Bo shrugged and found a table. Rance sat in the chair beside him, ordered a pitcher of beer and asked to see a menu. As Rance sat in silence once again, Bo studied the heavy beamed ceilings. The place was spectacular.

Their waitress, Payton, was back in no time with their drinks and menus. Pouring himself a beer, Bo perused the menu. Although the Grizzly offered a bit of everything, he immediately settled on the steak and potatoes. Setting the menu aside, he glanced around the room.

The music was too loud for general conversation, but not loud enough to dance. Not that it mattered. Rance didn't seem inclined to do either. Bo was actually pleased to see Payton weaving her way through the crowd towards their table. The quicker he could eat, the faster he could get home. Being patient with Rance was one thing, but sitting next to him in this current mood was quite another.

"You ready?" Payton asked.

"Yep. I'll take the ribeye with a loaded baked potato, carrots, and a side order of spinach, please."

As Rance ordered, Bo watched him carefully. The uptight manner in which he held himself was not about to prove to anyone in the room that yes, he actually was a gay man. What happened to the passionate lover of the previous night? Had coming back to the real world broken the spell?

Payton left to put their orders in, and Bo decided to engage Rance in conversation. Hell, anything better than feeling alone while on a date. Trying to speak over the music, he leaned closer to his lover. "Wanna dance?"

Rance studied the small dance floor and shook his head. "Maybe later. Music's a little too fast for my comfort."

Bo nodded, grinding his teeth. "I'll need help loading and unloading the hay this week."

Rance nodded. "You already told me that. I've scheduled Steve to give you a hand."

Well, so much for starting a conversation. He decided to try once more. "I've been thinking about joining The Gym. If you're interested, I think they give a discount for couples."

Rance shook his head. "I get enough exercise at work. Don't see the point in paying someone for what I can do for free in my own home."

Done. Bo didn't know what kind of bug crawled up Rance's ass, but he sure as hell didn't feel like playing the game just then. He spotted Asa Montgomery sitting at a table by himself and leaned back towards Rance.

"I'm gonna go ask Asa if Lynda and Jim can use his runway."

Rance acknowledged that he'd heard Bo, but said nothing.

With an irritated groan, he stood and made his way through the maze of tables. "Mr. Montgomery?"

Asa looked up from the paperwork he had spread out on the table. "Yes?"

"Sir, can I talk to you about something?" Although he'd never met Asa, he'd heard the man was a bit of a loner, preferring to stay holed-up in his large mansion on the edge of town. When Asa joined The Gym it seemed so out of character, it quickly became the buzz around town.

"Sure," Asa said, indicating a chair.

Bo took the offered seat. "We haven't met, but my name's Bo Lawson, and I do the farming at the Back Breaker ranch."

Asa nodded. "I've seen you in O'Brien's before. What can I do for you?"

"Well, sir, I recently found out I have a son, a baby boy named Joey. Anyway, the people who've been taking care of him are planning to bring him down from Canada this weekend."

"Yes?" Asa seemed to prod, no doubt wanting Bo to get on with his story and get the hell away from him.

"They're flying down in a private jet, and I wondered if it would be possible for them to use your landing strip instead of having to fly into Sheridan. I know it's a lot to ask, and I normally wouldn't have the balls to do such a thing, but I figured it couldn't hurt." There, he'd asked, like he'd told Jim he would.

"Sure. Call my office and they'll give you the coordinates and the runway specs."

"Just like that?" Bo was shocked. He thought he might have to do a bit of ass kissing to get Asa to agree to such a thing.

"Why not? The town council allowed me to put the damn thing in because I travel so much. The least I can do is make it available for other residents if they need it."

"Okay, great, thank you so much." Bo reached across the table, extending his hand.

Asa accepted the handshake with a grin. "Why do you seem afraid of me?"

Surprised by the question, Bo blinked several times. "Well, because you're Asa Montgomery, sir. You've been featured in every business and financial magazine out there."

Asa chuckled. "I'm just a guy from a small town in Kansas who happened to be in the right place at the right time. And the name's Asa."

Bo stood. "Thank you, again."

"You're welcome and congratulations on your son. Take care of him."

"I will." Feeling good, Bo walked back over to rejoin Rance. "That went well."

"That's good."

He'd barely sat down before Payton brought their food. "Mmm, smells good."

"Thank you," Rance said when Payton placed his prime rib in front of him.

Bo dug in to his meal, high on the thought of seeing Joey in a few days. If Rance wanted to be a stick in the mud, well so be it. Bo wasn't going to allow his lover's current mood to get him down. He ate with gusto and appreciation, making a mental note to bring Lynda, Jim and Neil here while they were in town.

"How's your food?" he asked Rance.

"Good, and yours?"

"Mine's good."

By the time they'd both finished, Bo was at the end of his rope. It was obvious by Rance's closed off mood there would be no dancing. Bo dug out his wallet and placed a couple of bills on the table. "You ready to go?"

"Yeah." Rance placed the money for his meal on the table and stood.

Evidently Bo'd been right about the dancing. He couldn't figure out what had changed on the drive up the mountain. If he pressed Rance for an answer would it backfire in his face?

He waited until they reached the bottom of the winding road before voicing his frustrations. From his seat beside the window, he turned to Rance. "I'm not sure what's going on, but I've got a feeling it's more than you're letting on."

Bo noticed the way Rance's hands tightened around the steering wheel before he answered. "I've already told you…"

"Yeah, I know, I have to be patient," Bo cut Rance off, tired of hearing the same old record.

"Well, if you know, then why can't you let it go?"

"Because I don't believe this has anything to do with your cock, that's why." He knew he was louder than the conversation warranted, but he was damn frustrated.

"It's not just my cock. It's everything. You, me, Joey. It's a lot to take in on a day's notice. If you can't give me some space while I work through it then we don't have much of a chance for a future."

Bo seethed. He had been prepared to work around Rance's body issues, but when his lover brought Joey into the mix, all bets were off. Even though Rance hadn't come out and said it, evidently raising a child wasn't something he was interested in. *Well, fuck you*, he mentally said to Rance.

Instead of breaking things off right there, Bo decided they both needed a few days to cool off. "Tell you what. You go ahead and do your brooding, thinking, whatever you call it, and I'll go on living. Maybe eventually you'll come to some kind of decision, but in the meantime, maybe it would be best if we don't see each other outside of work."

Rance chuckled in a bitter fashion. "You're sure quick to change your tune when things don't go your way."

Rance pulled into the Back Breaker and parked his truck. Bo tried to calm himself before saying something he'd regret later on.

"Quick? That's rich. I've been in love with you for a year and you know it. I've done the patient thing. I can't afford to put my life on hold indefinitely while you figure out whether or not I'm worthy."

When Rance didn't say anything right away, Bo grunted and got out. Walking towards the bunkhouse, he felt like he'd been sucker punched. *Fuck it.* He was tired of feeling like shit because of Rance.

* * * *

Rance punched the pillow, changing positions once again. When it was obvious he wasn't getting to sleep anytime soon, he swung his legs over the side of the bed and shuffled towards the kitchen and grabbed a bottle of beer.

He knew he'd screwed things up. He should've been honest and told Bo what was on his mind. Carrying the beer back to bed, Rance turned on the television.

A commercial for Montana tourism caught his eye. It depicted a father and son fishing and talked about slowing down and taking the time to enjoy family. "Damn, it's a conspiracy," he mumbled, shutting off the TV.

Rance knew his strange mood had given Bo ideas that weren't at all accurate, but what should he do about it? To confess that he was actually trying to decide whether or not to ask Bo and the baby to move in would leave him out on a limb. It wasn't that he didn't think the two of them could live together, but cohabitating would also mean Bo would see him naked.

He finished his beer and set the empty bottle on the bedside table. Sliding back under the sheet, he thought about the torture Bo had put him through over the previous year. How many times had he wanted Bo in his bed? Too many times to count.

As the months had gone by and his feelings for the bohemian farmer had grown deeper, he'd made himself keep his distance. After the previous night's passion, it was obvious Bo would accept Rance's physical deformities, but was he ready to expose himself?

In a rare move, Rance slid his hand down to his groin. He'd made a habit of sleeping in pyjama pants after the shooting to keep even himself from accidentally seeing his ruined cock.

As he ran his hand over the scarred, lumpy flesh he became hard. Rance tried to imagine what Bo would feel if he did the same. Would Bo know rubbing the scars gave Rance another level of excitement, that the ridges of tissue were more sensitive?

Rance shook his head and released his cock. What did it matter? He'd probably fucked things between them anyway. Tossing back the sheet, Rance got to his feet. *Maybe if I explain myself Bo will cut me some slack?*

He was almost to the front door when he realised the time. Maybe it would be best to at least wait until after breakfast. One thing was certain. He wanted Bo and Joey in his life. What difference could a few hours make?

* * * *

With new resolve, Rance walked towards the bunkhouse, hoping to talk to Bo before he started his day. A car pulling up beside his truck caught his attention however.

"Hey, what's up?" Rance asked Lark.

Lark settled the baseball cap on his head and withdrew a cooler from the back seat. "Just got back from taking Bo to the airport. He decided to fly up to Canada to get Joey instead of waiting for my folks to bring him here. Hope you don't mind, but he asked me to fill in while he's gone."

Rance's heart sunk. "How long will he be gone?"

Lark shrugged. "It's Bo. Who knows."

Lark started to walk off but stopped and turned to Rance. "He seemed pretty depressed. You wouldn't know anything about that, would you?"

Without answering, Rance strode towards his office in the barn. He'd heard too much about Sunrise

Gardens to feel comfortable with Bo's unplanned trip. Maybe he should hop on a plane and go after him?

Walking into his office, he was almost run over by Shep.

"It's about time you got here. We're gonna be late."

"Huh?" Rance asked.

"We've got the meeting in town with the Cattle Valley Days committee," Shep reminded him.

Shit, how could he have forgotten they were supposed to present their choices for the rodeo bulls? "Okay, let me grab the stock files."

"I'll be in the truck."

As Rance pawed through the stack of files on his shelf, he forced himself to get his head back into foreman mode. It wouldn't do to have a love-sick cowboy presenting to the committee.

Information in hand, Rance jogged towards Shep's pickup. "Sorry about that."

Shep pulled out of the drive and headed into town. "Do I need to even ask how your date went?"

"Probably not," Rance mumbled.

"Have anything to do with why I may have lost a damn good farmer?"

The file dropped to the floor of the truck as his heart skipped a beat. "What do you mean by that? I thought Bo just went to Canada to get Joey."

Shep seemed to study Rance for a few moments before answering. "All I know is he left a message on my cell phone saying he had to go. He said he hoped his job would be here when he got back, but he'd understand if I needed to hire a fulltime replacement before he returned."

Rance's head fell back against the seat. "I've really fucked stuff up, huh?"

"Wanna talk about it?"

"Not sure it'll do any good. We...um...got close on the overnight trip."

"Yeah, I figured that when I saw the two shredded sleeping bags zipped together. So what went wrong?"

"Nothing," Rance was quick to say, but the more he thought about it, the more depressed he became. "Everything."

"Well I know he didn't reject you. That wouldn't be something Bo had in him."

"No, he didn't reject me. He was wonderful when I told him what happened. I just wasn't ready to expose myself to him. I asked him to be patient, he agreed."

"So what's the problem?"

"Me. I started thinking, and I wanted to ask him and Joey to move in, but I got cold feet. We both know I tend to withdraw and clam up when that happens. I think Bo took it wrong though. By the end of our date, he was pissed and rightly so."

Shep pulled the truck to a stop in front of City Hall. "So what're you gonna do about it?"

"Wait for him to come back and beg for forgiveness?" Rance offered.

"Sure, if you want to put the fate of your relationship in someone else's hands. But as an alternative plan, why not go after him?"

Before Rance could fully think about it, Nate stepped out of the building.

"You coming?" Nate yelled.

Rance bent over and gathered the fallen file. "I'll give it some thought."

Shep joined Rance at the bottom of the steps. "Don't think too long. Bo's got more than just his own heart to worry about now. I imagine if he's worried about your feelings, he won't be in a hurry to put Joey in that situation."

Rance knew Shep was right, but he didn't have time to think about it just then. He followed his boss into the meeting room and took a seat. Expecting a smart-assed remark from Carol on their tardiness, Rance was surprised when it didn't come.

The woman across the table from him seemed to have her own problems to deal with. Several times during the first ten minutes, her focus seemed to be more on her cell phone than the meeting. Rance didn't know what the text messages said, but with each one she seemed to become more uptight.

After an hour's discussion of the rodeo events, they took a short coffee break. Rance noticed the way Nate led Carol quietly into an adjoining room.

"What do you think that's about?" Shep asked from beside him.

"No clue, but whatever it is, I'm sure Nate will handle it."

Shep nodded. "I've seen Carol pissed before, but I think this is something else. She almost looks sad, which would mean she actually has a heart behind that nice rack."

Shocked, Rance's jaw dropped. "Since when do you notice a woman's boobs?"

"Since I was born with eyes. Just because I don't feel like playing with them doesn't mean I don't appreciate 'em."

Rance couldn't say the same, so he shrugged instead. "I've got my own problems to deal with. I'll let Nate deal with Carol's."

"And I'm sure he'll deal with them in true Nate fashion," Shep chuckled.

Chapter Seven

Bo was having a fantastic dream about Rance when a hand groping his crotch woke him. He opened his eyes and grinned. "What the hell're you doing?"

"Well, I came out to tell you supper was ready, but it seemed as though you had other more urgent needs," Jim chuckled, gripping Bo's hard-on.

As good as the pressure felt, Bo wasn't about to proceed. Whether things worked out with Rance or not, it was Rance's hand he wanted shoved down the front of his jeans, not Jim's.

Bo brushed Jim's hand away. "Sorry, but you're the wrong guy for that job."

Jim sighed and got to his feet beside the hammock. "Shame to waste a perfectly good erection for a man so far away."

"Yeah, well my cock agrees with you, but the rest of me disagrees."

Bo flipped his way out of the hammock and kissed Jim on the cheek. "It's no reflection on your skills as a lover, believe me."

"Now you're just trying to make me feel better," Jim pouted.

Laughing, Bo wrapped his arm around his old friend as they headed inside. "Maybe."

Before he could have a seat at the table, the house phone rang. "Want me to get it?"

"If you would," Jim answered, setting a platter of roast and vegetables on the table.

Bo walked into the living room and picked up the phone. "Hello?"

"Hey, just the guy I was looking for," Randy, the guard at the front gate, said.

Smiling, Bo shook his head. "I told you when I got in that this was a business trip, not a pleasure trip."

"Funny. I'm not after your dick, well I am, but that's not why I'm calling. There's some guy here that says he needs to speak to you."

Bo's jaw dropped. The first person he thought of was Joey's biological father suddenly showing up. "Who is it?"

"A hot cowboy all duded up in black, says his name is Rance."

Bo's heart jumped for joy. "I'll be right there."

Hanging up the phone, Bo strode into the kitchen. "That was Randy on the phone. Rance is at the gate."

Jim whistled. "He must've picked up on that dream you were obviously having earlier."

Rolling his eyes, Bo bent to kiss his son on top of the head. "Don't hold dinner. I've got a few things to work out before I can bring Rance back to meet Joey."

Lynda grinned and kissed him on the cheek. "Good luck, sweetie."

"Thanks."

Jogging towards the golf cart, Bo ran his fingers through his hair. It had been four days since he'd last seen Rance. Maybe he should run upstairs and shave?

Quickly rejecting the idea, he hopped into the cart and took off. He hoped like hell Rance showing up was a good sign. Surely if he was being fired, Shep would've called.

As he neared the gate, the sight of the good-looking cowboy hardened his cock once more. Damn, that was one fine looking man.

"Hey," he greeted, pulling to a stop. He didn't dare make a move without a sign from Rance.

"Sorry for just showing up like this, but I need to talk to you." Rance gestured to the small duffle at his feet. "You mind?"

"Not at all. Hop in."

As soon as Rance was settled, Bo headed towards his favourite spot by the lake. When Rance didn't say anything, Bo decided to start off the conversation. "So, what brings you all the way to Canada?"

"Don't be a dumbass. You know I came for you."

Bo slowed the cart to a stop and turned off the battery. "I don't really think I'm the one being the dumbass, do you?"

Rance took off his hat and tossed it into the backseat. "No. I know perfectly well who the ass has been. But in my own defence, I think you took my mood the other night to mean more than it did."

"What the hell else was I supposed to think? You asked me out, and then practically ignored me all night. I had more conversation with the damn waitress than I had with you."

"I know, but I had a lot of things on my mind." Before Bo could say anything, Rance held up a hand. "And yes, I should've discussed them with you, but before I could work up the nerve you got pissed off and flew up here."

Bo shook his head. "It wasn't about being pissed, hurt maybe, but not pissed."

Now that Bo had the chance to pull Rance into a conversation about their date, he wasn't about to pass it up. "I understood that you needed time, but what hurt was you shutting me out completely."

"I know, and I knew it that night. I thought I'd be able to talk to you about it the following morning, but you were already gone."

Bo shrugged. "I felt the need to be around people who loved me."

Rance reached over and put his hand on Bo's thigh. "You could've stayed on the ranch and received that if only you'd believed in me."

Closing his eyes, Bo leaned towards Rance. Brushing his lover's lips with his own, he opened his eyes. "Are you saying you love me?"

Pulling Bo closer, Rance took the kiss deeper. Bo melted at the tender way Rance's fingers threaded through his hair.

Breaking the kiss, Rance stared into Bo's eyes. "I've loved you for a long time. I was just too scared to admit it."

Bo put his hand over the bulge in Rance's jeans. "And this?"

"That loves you, too."

Bo grinned. "You know that's not what I'm talking about."

"Yeah, I know."

"So?" Bo prodded.

"Okay, here's the thing. I want you and Joey to come back to the ranch and live with me. The problem is I'm not sure if I'm ready to expose myself to you." Rance took a deep breath. "There, I've said it."

It finally made sense to Bo why Rance had acted like an ass on their date. His lover had been doing a lot of heavy thinking. Bo wanted to spend the rest of his life with Rance, but…

"Until you trust me enough to share yourself, body and soul, I can't live with you."

"It's not a matter of trust," Rance tried to say.

"Yes, it is. Your dick is ugly, so what? If you think that's what's most important to me, then you really don't know me at all."

"Really? How many different men have you fucked over your lifetime?" Rance challenged.

Bo reared back as if he'd been slapped. Knowing that he'd told Rance about his past, he couldn't believe the man had the nerve to ask the question. "Fuck you, you sonofabitch."

Rance held up his hands to stop Bo's tirade. "All I'm saying is you're used to sex a certain way. A way I'm not sure I can even give you."

"You did a pretty good imitation of it the other night."

Rance shook his head. "I can get hard, I can even come, thank God, but I haven't fucked anyone since the shooting. I…"

Bo stopped Rance with a kiss. Why did the guy insist on putting so much pressure on himself? Bo finished the kiss and climbed out of the golf cart. Walking to the water's edge, he crossed his arms and turned back to Rance.

"What do you tell someone who gets thrown from a horse?"

"Huh? I tell 'em to get right back on, but what does that have to do with anything. I was shot. I didn't fall off a damn horse."

"It's the same thing if you'd take the time to think about it," Bo tried to tell him.

The expression on Rance's face told Bo he wasn't buying it. "Look, I like to fuck, even more than getting fucked, but that's beside the point. Whether you can or can't doesn't matter to me. I think you're making a mountain out of a mole hill. So fucking strip already."

Rance's eyes rounded. "What?"

"You heard me, strip. Take the jump. Stop trying to talk yourself out of this relationship."

"I'm not doing that," Rance argued.

"You damn sure are. And I can see it driving a wedge between us. So, strip. If you trust me, you'll just do it."

Rance's jaw snapped shut. With narrowed eyes, he got out of the cart and stalked towards Bo. "You wanna see what I can't even bear to look at? Fine, but don't say I didn't warn you."

Rance reached down and unfastened his jeans. He bent over and pushed the denim along with his underwear to his ankles. With an expression Bo couldn't read, he crossed his arms.

Though he'd asked for it, Bo hadn't been mentally prepared for the sight of Rance's cock. He quickly schooled his shock and stepped forward. Kneeling in front of his lover, he took the flaccid shaft in his hand, seeing Rance's muscles tense.

He felt he owed it to Rance to thoroughly inspect the damaged member. Thick scars intersected midway up the length, giving the cock the appearance that it had indeed been surgically reattached.

Leaning forward, he began kissing the more prominent scars. As he did, the cock in his hand began to lengthen. Bo smiled as he continued to soothe the savage beast standing in front of him.

Hard, it was easy to see why Rance worried about his ability to fuck. The head and about three inches of the shaft jutted out at an unnatural angle. Gazing up into Rance's eyes, Bo grinned. He knew Rance would know if he lied, so he decided to tell his partner exactly what he thought.

"Well, you were right. It is an ugly fucker, but guess what?"

Rance continued to stare down at him, not saying a word.

"It doesn't change my feelings for you one damn bit."

He reached up and pulled Rance to his knees. With his lover now at eye level, Bo kissed him, hoping like hell he'd passed whatever test Rance needed as proof of his feelings.

The swipe of Rance's tongue across Bo's lips gave him the answer he sought. Putting all the love he felt into the kiss, Bo opened and moaned. The issues with Rance's body image would take time, but he now knew his lover trusted him. He'd take that over a perfect cock any day.

* * * *

Rance ground his erection against Bo's. "Take me somewhere and make love to me."

Releasing him, Bo grinned. "I can do that."

As Rance watched, Bo quickly stripped out of his clothes. "What're you doing?"

Digging a condom out of his wallet, Bo reached for Rance's shirt. "I thought we were going to make love?"

"Here?"

Bo chuckled. "This is the perfect place. You'll find out when I take you to meet the others, Sunrise Garden's is special."

After making sure no one else was around, Rance stepped out of his shoes, jeans and underwear. He'd never had sex in a semi-public place, and the idea secretly thrilled him. He stretched out in the soft grass and waited for Bo to join him.

The erection bobbing above him did more than anything to prove that Bo wasn't disgusted as he'd feared. Spreading his thighs in invitation, Rance held out his arms and welcomed the weight of his lover's body as it covered him. Rance didn't need to remind Bo it had been years since he'd had sex. His lover held fingers in front of Rance's mouth. Opening, Rance thoroughly bathed the long, graceful digits in his own saliva.

Bo quirked an eyebrow. "Damn, keep that up and I'll blow before I even suit up."

Chuckling, Rance released Bo's fingers. "Can't have that."

Bo leaned down for a kiss as his fingers began to explore Rance's puckered hole. *Fuck.* Rance had forgotten how good it felt to be stretched. His body opened for Bo's penetrating touch as he softly nipped his lover's bottom lip.

Adding another finger, Bo gave him a worried expression. "You probably shouldn't do that. You could get carried away and draw blood."

Running his fingers through Bo's silky hair, Rance shook his head. "I'm not going to live my life afraid to touch and love you. I won't purposely do anything stupid, but I won't police my every action either."

"Do you have any idea what it would do to me if you contracted this damn virus?" Bo asked.

"We need to get something straight between us before we go any further. I'm choosing to make love with you, knowing full well what could happen. If for some reason I contract HIV I don't want you to feel guilty. I'm a big boy. I know the risks involved, and I'm willing to accept them in order to be with you."

Bo shook his head. "You shouldn't have to."

"But I do, and I have. So open up that condom and fuck me already."

Bo slid back and came to rest on his knees between Rance's spread thighs. Reaching for the foil packet, he sheathed his erection. Rance knew his lover was still worried, but Rance also knew he had a lifetime to convince him that he'd accepted the consequences.

Positioning the crown of his cock at Rance's entrance, Bo began to rock back and forth until the head breached Rance's hole. The hesitation in Bo's surge forward told Rance his lover was still thinking too much.

"After the shooting I thought my life was over. I lived every day as if I were already dead. You changed that for me. A single year with you and Joey means more to me than a lifetime of being alone."

With a thrust of his hips, Bo buried himself inside Rance's body. The burn took his breath away as he patiently waited for his body to become accustomed to Bo's cock.

Closing his eyes, Rance moaned as the ache soon gave way to pure pleasure. "God, you feel good."

"Not half as good as you," Bo grunted, pulling out slowly before sinking back in.

Hooking his arms under his knees, Rance opened himself further. Without lube, he had no doubt he'd be sore as hell by the time Bo was finished with him, but he couldn't have cared less. Truly making love for the first time in his eventful life was worth every ounce of discomfort.

Gazing up into Bo's dark eyes, he wondered how he could've ever been fooled by Oren. Never had his ex-boyfriend looked at him the way Bo did.

Bo surprised him by reaching between them and fisting Rance's cock.

"You don't have to," Rance was quick to say.

"Relax. I want to," Bo whispered, his hips moving in time with his hand.

How long had it been since someone had touched him? Hell, for that matter, how long since he'd even had the nerve to pleasure himself?

"Stay with me," Bo panted, picking up speed.

Rance felt Bo's thumb press against the thick scar just under the head of his cock. "Fuck!" he screamed as his shaft erupted in ropes of thick white cum, painting not only his chest but Bo's as well.

Raising his face to the setting sun, Bo roared as his climax overtook him. Rance was in awe of the power his lover exhibited in the pumped muscles and chorded tendons on display. *Damn, I'm one lucky sonofabitch.*

Lowering himself, Bo began licking his way down Rance's stomach, tasting the seed spilled earlier. Fisting his lover's hair, Rance's mouth watered as Bo noisily enjoyed the taste of cum. "I wish…"

Bo's finger covered Rance's lips. "Shhh, I'll share some of your own with you."

Rance blinked, unaccustomed to someone being able to read him so clearly. Yeah, he wished he could lick every inch of the man poised over him, including the life-threatening essence. Rance wondered if making love to an HIV positive man would always leave him to feel like he was missing out on something.

The sex was fantastic, but it was the before and after play that seemed to be so one-sided. What would it be like to put Bo's naked cock into his mouth and pleasure him to completion? Rance knew it would never happen. With Bo there would be no unprotected sex of any kind, including blow-jobs and rimming. He'd heard about the whole plastic wrap thing, but that wasn't the same as being able to taste the man you loved.

"What's wrong?" Bo asked, crawling up Rance's body to kiss him.

"Nothing," Rance answered, licking Bo's lips.

"Liar."

Rance knew he needed to be honest with Bo. "I just realised all the implications of making love to someone with HIV."

Bo's body tensed. "Will the dangers be too much for you?"

Rance shook his head. "No. It just seems so one sided. There are so many things I'd like to do to you, but I know I can't. I guess I'm like the boy in the proverbial candy store who wants everything and is told he must only pick from a certain rack."

Bo rolled off Rance and took care of the condom, tying it off and stuffing it into the pocket of his shorts. Getting to his feet, Bo walked to the golf cart and extracted a tissue from the centre console.

Rance watched his lover, trying to discern Bo's mood. "Did I hurt your feelings or piss you off?"

Bo returned to his position beside Rance. "Neither. Just worries me."

"How so?" Rance asked.

"Will I be enough? Is what I'm able to give you enough?"

Rance's heart melted. He'd been so caught up in what he couldn't have with Bo, he'd forgotten to take into account the most important thing that he did receive.

Reaching out, Rance pulled Bo into his arms and kissed him. "Loving you, becoming a family with you and Joey is more important to me than anything. Please don't let my whining lead you to believe anything different. It's a new way of making love, that's all. I just wish I could bring you the same pleasure you bring me."

Bo grinned. "No worries there."

It seemed as though Bo wanted to say something else, but he snapped his mouth closed and shook his head.

"What?"

After several long moments, Bo buried his face against Rance's neck. "The day I found out I was positive was the worst day of my life."

"That's understandable," Rance cut in.

Bo nodded. "I suppose, but it wasn't the threat of getting AIDS that scared me. I was damaged goods. What decent man would want someone like me for a life partner? So, I fucked. And I fucked. And I fucked some more. Always safely, but never allowing myself to get attached."

"Oh, babe," Rance soothed, kissing the top of Bo's head.

"When Lark and Kade came up to visit last year, I saw the two of them together and knew I wanted what they had. I thought it was an impossible dream, but I decided that sex wasn't enough for me anymore."

Bo looked up into Rance's eyes. "You're the first person to ever truly love me."

Rance felt the need to open his soul to the man in his arms. For too long he'd allowed himself to live the life of a victim, always afraid of what someone might think of him. "I think we're more alike than you realise. For you it was contracting HIV, for me it was being shot. Both of us thought we were too damaged to be loved."

"And now we have each other."

"And Joey," Rance added. "Speaking of which, when am I gonna get the chance to meet the newest addition to our family?"

Bo's entire face lit up. "Right now."

They both reached for their clothes at the same time and began to dress. Bo was almost vibrating with excitement as he struggled with his shirt.

"Wait until you see him. He's absolutely perfect."

Rance chuckled and climbed into the golf cart. "As you've already shown me, perfect is in the eye of the beholder. So I have absolutely no doubts our Joey is perfect."

* * * *

After giving his hands a good scrubbing in the kitchen sink, Bo led Rance into the living room. Sitting in front of the TV, Neil's boxer-briefs were around his ankles as Jim lazily sucked his cock.

Rolling his eyes, Bo cleared his throat. Jim eventually pulled his mouth from Neil's shaft and smiled.

"You must be Rance," Jim greeted.

"Yep," Rance answered.

Bo wrapped an arm around Rance. His lover seemed a bit unnerved by Jim and Neil's apparent lack of modesty. Bo would have to remember to ask Jim and Neil to cool things a bit while Rance was in the house.

"Where's Joey?" Bo asked.

"Upstairs. Lynda's getting him into his pyjamas." Neil gestured towards a chair. "Have a seat."

Bo shook his head. "Thanks, but I think I'll take Rance up and introduce him to Lynda and Joey."

He started to lead Rance through the living room. He stopped beside the sofa and whispered in Jim's ear. "Do me a favour and try to finish before we get back down."

Laughing, Jim nodded. "No problem."

As soon as they were out of sight, Bo pulled Rance into his arms and kissed him. "Sorry if that made you uncomfortable. Things are a little different around here."

"I guess so. I mean, I've heard stories, but...wow."

Chuckling, Bo continued to lead Rance upstairs. Stepping into the room, Bo's heart melted like it did every time he looked at his son.

"Is he asleep?" Bo asked Lynda.

"No, but he's not far from it." Lynda rose from a rocking chair and gently handed Joey to Bo.

"I'd like you to meet Rance," Bo introduced, not taking his eyes from Joey's sweet face.

"Nice to finally meet you." Instead of shaking Rance's hand, Lynda cupped his cheek in greeting.

"Likewise. Thanks for taking care of Bo and Joey for me."

Bo probably should have been offended by the way Rance said it, but he felt nothing but warmth at the words.

"It's been my absolute pleasure," Lynda answered. "I'll leave the three of you alone. Come down once you get Joey to bed and have something to eat."

Bo nodded his agreement and Lynda left the room. Turning to Rance, he held out his son. "Would you like to hold him?"

Rance bit his lip and nodded. "Let me sit down first."

After taking a seat in the rocking chair, Bo placed Joey in Rance's arms. Joey gave a little start as his eyes opened, but quickly settled back down.

"He's beautiful," Rance whispered, running his index finger over Joey's long black lashes.

"What, you didn't believe me when I told you earlier how perfect he was?" Bo teased, kneeling in front of Rance and Joey.

Rance leaned down and placed a soft kiss on Joey's forehead. "I didn't think it was possible. Can I ask a personal question?"

"Sure. I've got no secrets."

"Is his biological father Native American?"

"According to Jan, he was, but she didn't know what tribe or anything. Hell, she didn't even know the guys last name, only that he went by Hawk and they met at some sex party she attended. It's a shame really. Joey will probably never know his true ancestry."

Rance shook his head. "If there comes a time when Joey wants to know, we'll help him. I imagine there are tests or something that can be done. In the meantime, we'll give him all the love and self-confidence any child could ask for."

"You got that right."

Chapter Eight

After stacking the last bale into the hay barn, Bo took off towards the house. Although he still had two hours before the baptism, Bo was hoping to stop by the reception room to see if Tyler needed any help getting the room ready.

It had worked out perfectly when he and Rance had run into Tyler and Hearn at O'Brien's on Tuesday. They'd mentioned getting Joey baptised and Tyler had suggested a dual baptism with Gracie the following Sunday evening.

"I'm home," Bo called, entering the house he and Joey shared with Rance.

"Back here."

Bo pulled the sweaty T-shirt over his head as he made his way to the bedroom. "I'm just gonna jump in the shower..."

Bo's voice trailed off as he took in the sight in front of him. Rance was spread eagle on the bed with his hand wrapped around his cock. More than anything it was the growing acceptance Rance had over his own body image that told Bo how much his lover trusted him.

"Well, hello." Bo gazed at Rance's cock as he stripped.

"Been waiting for you."

"I can see that. Give me a second to wash the stink off, and I'll be more than happy to take over for you."

"I don't mind stink," Rance informed him, spreading his legs further apart.

Bo grinned. "Where's Joey?"

"The boys have him over at the bunkhouse."

As much as he wanted to bury himself in the ass on display, Bo was more interested in the cock currently being stroked to full hardness. They'd been back from Canada for over a week, and ever since he'd wanted to be filled by that particular appendage, but had put off saying anything. He knew the last thing Rance needed was to be reminded of his injury, but Bo was sure they could make it work.

Retrieving the bottle of lube and two condoms from the drawer, he knelt on the side of the bed.

"Fuck me," he finally begged his lover.

Rance's eyes shot wide open. "What?"

"You heard me."

Rance blinked several times before lowering his eyes. "I don't think I can."

Bo watched Rance's newfound self confidence begin to wane. No, that definitely wasn't an option. Pulling his lover into his arms, Bo gave Rance a passionate kiss. "I think you can. But even if it doesn't work out, we'll be fine."

Rance gave him a short nod of acceptance, but Bo could tell his partner was still uneasy. Positioning himself on the bed, Bo squirted some lube onto his fingers and reached between his legs.

Bo was no stranger to the allure of butt plugs, often inserting them before a long day on the tractor, so the process of stretching himself went fairly quickly. He watched as Rance struggled to get the condom rolled down his shaft. Bo had a feeling it had more to do with the fact Rance wasn't as hard as he'd been earlier rather than the awkward curve his cock took midpoint.

Reaching out, Bo removed Rance's frustrated, fumbling hands. "Let me help."

He began running his fingers up and down Rance's length, taking time to appreciate the heavy ball that had centred and now hung between his partner's legs. With the crown of Rance's cock safely sheathed, Bo leaned forward and sucked the head into his mouth. He smiled around the growing erection and smoothly slid the rest of the condom past the odd angle and down as far as it would go.

Task complete, he sat up and rolled a condom down his own length, never could he take too many safety precautions to protect his family. "I think it'll be better if I'm on all fours."

Bo got into position and Rance knelt behind him. With his ass well-lubed, the first half of Rance's cock slid in without too much discomfort. The scarring Rance had sustained made his cock much thicker than the plugs Bo had been using, but it was a pleasant ache.

When Rance reached the main injury site, he shifted to raise himself behind Bo.

"Tell me if I start to hurt you."

Rance slowly buried more of his cock. Holding his breath, Bo almost came on the spot when the crooked penis rubbed against his prostate.

"Fuck, babe, I think I've just discovered heaven," he panted as more of Rance's cock was fed slowly into him.

Rance hadn't even fully seated himself before Bo lost the fight on his control. Bo's entire body began to convulse at the intensity of his orgasm. Through every quake, Rance's cock continued its assault on Bo's prostate.

With his ass still in the air, Bo gripped the base of the condom, knowing he wasn't quite finished yet. *Damn.* Why hadn't he realised Rance's cock would be at the perfect angle to give so much pleasure?

The answer came to him immediately. Because they both had been so focused on the cosmetic appearance of Rance's cock they hadn't thought of anything beyond that. If ever the saying, 'Looks could be deceiving' were true, it was in the case of Rance's scarred cock.

"You okay?" Rance asked, when Bo's breathing returned to normal.

"Fuck, no, I'm not okay," Bo answered. "Never in my life have I felt anything like it."

"Want me to pull out?"

"Hell, no. I want you to fuck me like you mean it."

Rance's hand came down hard on Bo's ass. "You asked for it."

By the time Rance had a steady rhythm going, Bo couldn't seem to get enough air into his lungs. The constant stimulation of his prostate was overwhelming, almost to the point of true pain.

Rance yelled Bo's name as he plunged in once more and came. Unable to breathe, Bo gave Rance a nudge until his lover got the hint, pulled out and collapsed to the side.

Squeezing his eyes shut, Bo tried like hell to regain his faculties. Jesus Christ he'd never experienced anything like that.

He wasn't sure how long he lay there, but eventually he turned his head to face Rance. His lover appeared to be sound asleep. Evidently he hadn't been the only one affected by the intense session.

His hand around the base of his cock reminded Bo he needed to dispose of the condoms. As much as he hated to move, he made himself trudge towards the bathroom.

After cleaning himself, he took a washcloth back into the bedroom and removed the condom from Rance's flaccid cock. He couldn't help but chuckle at the amount of ejaculate present. "Poor baby's probably dehydrated now."

Rance stirred as Bo bathed his groin. "Shit, what time is it?"

"Relax. We've got over an hour before we need to leave."

Settling back down onto the mattress, Rance sighed. "That was nice."

Laughing, Bo leaned down and kissed Rance's temple. "That my love, was heaven and hell combined. I don't know that my heart could take it all the time, but I definitely plan on doing it again."

* * * *

Rance whistled as Bo came out of the bedroom dressed in his new black suit. The only thing off about his lover was the way Bo had his hair tied at the nape of his neck. He knew his partner was trying to look respectable, but then, it just wasn't the man he'd fallen head-over-heels in love with.

"You look good enough to eat," Rance told Bo, giving him a hug.

"I feel kinda silly," Bo admitted, pulling at his starched white collar.

"Maybe this'll help." Rance reached up and pulled the leather thong from Bo's hair. The soft strands fanned over Bo's shoulder. "Yep, that's better."

Bo grinned. "Feels a lot better, too."

"You ready?" Rance asked, running his hands over Bo's tight ass. He still hadn't fully recovered from the pleasure of being buried inside Bo.

"Yeah. Let's hope the guys managed to get Joey changed into the outfit you sent over."

"I wouldn't count on it."

They made their way to the bunkhouse, only stopping twice for kisses. Rance couldn't seem to keep his hands off Bo's ass. Damn, he'd turned into a sex maniac in the last few hours.

The way Bo continued to brush his hand across the front of Rance's fly, Rance had a feeling he wasn't the only afternoon convert.

Walking into the bunkhouse, Rance's jaw dropped. Joey was in the pristine white outfit Lynda had sent from Canada. Not only was he spotless, but it appeared his cowboys were taking their job as babysitters seriously.

Joey was sitting up in the centre of a blanket with pillows surrounding him. Jim, Steve and Buddy were dressed in suits, sitting cross-legged on the floor as well. Steve had a burp cloth in his hand ready to catch any escaping drool, Buddy had Joey's stuffed frog, trying his best to entertain the little guy, and Jim had a bottle and diapers at the ready in case they were needed.

Bo bumped Rance with his hip. "See? No need to worry."

Rance chuckled at the goofy grins plastered on the faces of the rough-stock cowboys. "I never thought I'd live to see the day."

Stepping over the circle of pillows meant to be some sort of barricade, Rance picked Joey up. "How's daddy's boy?"

Joey smiled as he reached for Rance's hat. Rance pulled his head back enough to keep the hat on his head. "You ready to go to your first party?"

The cowboys stood and brushed off their dress clothes. "I changed him about twenty minutes ago," Jim informed Rance.

"Good. Thanks, guys. You can baby-sit anytime."

"We'll hold ya to that," Buddy piped up.

* * * *

Except for Joey filling his diaper halfway through the service, everything went off without a hitch. Bo and Rance took turns holding Joey, while the army of Godfather's stood behind them. Bo knew Joey was lucky. Instead of one Godparent, Joey had seven men willing to step in and take over care of him should anything ever happen to Rance or Bo.

As his friends from Cattle Valley began filtering over to the reception hall, Bo passed Joey off to Uncle Lark. "We'll be in shortly."

Lark nodded and proudly escorted Joey to his party. Bo turned and pulled Rance into his arms. Standing at the front of the church, he kissed him. "After the farce of my marriage to Jan, I promised myself never to do it again. But loving you has changed my way of thinking."

Rance cocked his head to the side. "You saying you want to get married?"

"Yep. Right here, right now. I don't need anyone but you me and God to do it. A traditional ceremony is all about the ceremony. I want this to just be about the two of us and our love for each other."

Rance buried his fingers in Bo's hair and gave him a kiss as soft as an angel's wing. "I Rance Benning, take you, Bo Lawson, to be my husband. I will cherish and protect you all the days of my life."

Though it was short and sweet, Bo felt himself getting misty-eyed. "The day I saw you in the bakery was the day my heart began truly beating for the first time in my life. I don't know what I've done to deserve you, and to be honest, you'll probably never convince me that I do, but I thank you. You, Rance Benning, are the only lover and partner I'll ever need."

Their kiss following their impromptu ceremony was more sexual than sweet. Bo couldn't seem to pull Rance close enough to satisfy him. Their tongues duelled and fucked each other's mouths as Rance slid his leg up to wrap around Bo's hip.

"No sex in the church," Reverend Sharp chuckled from the doorway.

Breaking the kiss, Bo glanced over his shoulder at Casey. "Give us a break, we just got married."

"What?" Casey walked further into the sanctuary. "Congratulations."

"You're not mad that we did it without you, are you?" Rance asked.

Reverend Sharp shook his head. Casey leaned forward and gave them both a hug and kiss on the cheek. "You had the most important witness. That's all that matters."

"My thoughts exactly." Bo took Rance's hand and pulled him towards the door to the hall. "Let's celebrate."

Because of their earlier activities, he hadn't been able to stop into the hall before the service. Bo stopped just inside the door in awe of Tyler's decorating. Gazing around the room at all the white draped fabric with pink and blue accents he shook his head. "Does the man do anything half-way?"

"He wouldn't be Tyler if he did," Rance answered squeezing Bo's hand.

They joined the crowd in search of their son. Rance spotted Joey first, pointing him out. "There he is."

Bo rolled his eyes. "Hell, we'll never get him back."

Joey was safely perched on Gill's massive forearm, pulling on the man's ears as everyone around them laughed, including the ex-football player.

"Looks like there's a line," Rance said, pointing to the left of Gill.

Resigned to sharing his son, Bo led Rance over to the food table. Sean O'Brien was setting out another pan of lasagne as Bo picked up a plate. "Looks good, Sean."

"It is. Jay's a damn good cook. A hell of a lot better than I am."

Bo's eyes strayed to the quiet man in the kitchen. He didn't know much about the newcomer, but then again, he doubted many did. Other than Nate, Jay tended to keep to himself. Although he had to admit, the guy appeared to be a lot happier than when he'd first arrived in town.

Filling his plate, Bo found two empty seats next to Isaac, Matt and Sam. "Mind if we join you?"

"Not at all," Sam replied.

Rance gestured to the three men. "It's rare to see the three of you out together."

Isaac finished swallowing a bite of food before responding. "Yeah. We finally decided to hire someone to fill in on the weekends for us."

"Really? Someone from Cattle Valley?" Bo asked.

"No. Daniel was one of my professors. We kept in touch after graduation, and when he mentioned breaking away from the university, I suggested he come here," Matt informed them.

"Well, we can always use another doctor in town." Pointing towards his lasagne, Bo rolled his eyes. "This is a little bit of heaven on a plate."

"You haven't tried the tiramisu yet," Rance said, shovelling a bite into his mouth.

"No, but I'm about to." Bo leaned over and thrust his tongue into Rance's mouth. The taste of espresso mixed with cocoa teased his taste buds. "Mmm, more."

Laughing, Rance fed him a bit of his dessert. "This is, like, our wedding cake."

"What? You two got married?" Isaac asked.

Bo swallowed the delectable sweet before answering. "Just a few minutes ago actually."

"Why didn't you tell anyone?" Isaac probed further.

Bo looked at Rance and shrugged. "It was just the two of us. The way we wanted it."

Isaac nodded. "Then congratulations."

"Thanks." Bo squeezed Rance's thigh under the table.

A cry sounded from across the room. Both Rance and Bo shot to their feet. The other men at their table started to chuckle. Bo blew them a raspberry and took off, Rance in tow. The problem was evident the closer they got to Joey.

Their sweet baby boy was desperately trying to climb out of Erico's arms. Before Bo could reach them, Jay stepped up and extracted the screaming child from Erico's grasp. Joey settled immediately against Jay's thin chest and stuck his thumb in his mouth.

Rance started to pass Bo, but he reached out and pulled his new husband to a stop. "Have you ever seen Jay look that happy?"

Rance seemed to study the androgynous-looking man. "No, I don't believe I have."

Jay kissed the top of Joey's head as he walked with the baby towards the corner of the room. Erico was left looking slightly unnerved. Bo wondered if the master chef had ever been put in his place quite so blatantly and by someone as sweet and quiet as Jay.

"Let's leave 'em be for now," Bo whispered in Rance's ear.

Rance nodded. "I think we've found the perfect babysitter."

"More perfect than a bunkhouse full of rowdy cowboys?" Bo joked.

"Well, maybe we can reserve Jay for those special occasions when the cowboys are whooping it up on the town."

"Yeah, like next month's rodeo. Shit, maybe we'd better get our bid in early. I saw the way Hearn's eyes lit up when Jay took the baby from Erico. You can't tell me that man doesn't have designs on our babysitter."

Rance laughed and gave Bo a loud smacking kiss. "Go get 'em, tiger."

Crossing the room to the quiet corner Jay had retreated to, Bo advanced slowly. The young man seemed easily startled for what ever reason, and the last thing Bo wanted was to cause Jay to drop Joey.

He stood back a good ten feet and waited for Jay to notice him. Although it was hard to hear over the noise of the partying crowd, Bo caught snippets of *Hush, Little Baby*, sung in Jay's soft calming voice. The tone was so perfect, it brought tears to Bo's eyes. What the hell was this kid doing working in a bar as a cook?

The song ended, snapping Bo out of his trance. When he glanced up Jay was staring at him. "I'm sorry. I hope it's okay. He was crying and…"

"It's fine. More than fine actually. You're amazing with him." Bo stepped forward and ran a hand over Joey's back. His poor little guy was sound asleep. "Rance and I were wondering if you'd be interested in sitting for us occasionally."

"Me?"

Bo smiled at the shocked expression on Jay's face. "Yes, you. From what I can tell, Joey already trusts you, so why shouldn't we?"

Jay gazed down at the sleeping face pressed against his chest. "I'd like that very much."

"Good. I don't know if anyone's told you about the Cattle Valley Days coming up the first part of July, but there's a Saturday night street dance that Rance and I would like to attend, if you're free to stay with Joey."

Jay nodded. "I can do that. I hadn't planned on going anyway."

Strong arms wrapped around Bo's waist. "You about ready to head home? I've already said our goodbyes. I told them I was hot to get you into our honeymoon bed."

Bo turned his head to the side and kissed his partner. "Just about."

Regarding Jay once again, Bo stepped forward. "Time to take the big boy home."

Jay kissed Joey's forehead again before handing him off to Bo. "If you can hold on a minute, I'll write down my phone number."

"Sure." Bo settled Joey on his shoulder. Once Jay had fled to find a scrap of paper, Bo walked back over to Rance. "You should've heard him singing to Joey."

"Good?"

"Better than good." Bo led his family towards the door. He hated to be a party pooper, but his day had started early, and he had another one starting at six in the morning. The trip to Canada had set his schedule back a few days. Lark was good, but he simply wasn't as strong as Bo.

Jay met them near the door. "That's the number for O'Brien's. I work there most nights, so you should be able to reach me. I'm hoping to get a phone soon, so when I do I'll make sure you get that number as well."

Bo thanked him again and they headed to the truck. "Have you ever heard Jay talk that much?"

"No, can't say as I have," Rance answered.

After getting Joey buckled into his car seat, Rance pulled out of the parking lot. "By the way, Shep said for you to sleep in, that Sundays weren't meant for working."

Bo grinned. He knew there was a reason he liked his boss. "I wonder if we could find someone to take Joey for a couple hours in the afternoon."

"Probably, why, what've you got in mind?"

Reaching across the back of the seat, Bo tickled the back of his partner's neck. "Oh, I've still got a few tricks up my sleeve."

CATTLE VALLEY
DAYS

Dedication

For M. Todd Howell
Maybe someday we'll get lucky and a place like
Cattle Valley will really exist.

Chapter One

Entering the house, Nate tossed his keys onto the table and sighed. With the annual Cattle Valley Days only a week away, his work day was getting longer and longer. Whose idea was it for him to run for Mayor?

He chuckled. *Me, myself and I. Suck it up, Mayor Gills.*

Nate set his briefcase down and headed for the kitchen. Hopefully his men had saved him some dinner. An item of underwear in the middle of the great room caught his attention. Suddenly his good mood went south.

"Dammit! Can't you pigs clean up after yourselves once in a while?"

A chuckling Rio appeared in the doorway leading from the media room. "You're home. I thought maybe you forgot the way."

Nate was too tired to get into the ongoing discussion about the hours he'd been keeping. He pointed towards the red boxer-briefs. "Why the hell are your dirty drawers on the floor?"

Rio walked over and snatched the underwear into his hand. "Sorry. Must've fallen out of the basket on the way to the laundry room."

Nate sighed. "Did you at least leave me something for dinner?"

Rio held up his hands. "You said you'd grab something. Ryan and I went to O'Brien's for Taco Tuesday. I can make you an omelette or a sandwich."

Nate was so tired he couldn't even remember having a conversation about dinner. "Forget it. I'm going to bed."

He walked upstairs shaking his head. Maybe a decent night's sleep would put him in a better frame of mind. His footsteps slowed as he neared the guest room. Would Rio and Ryan feel slighted if he slept by himself? Yeah, probably, but he was too worn out to care.

He shed his clothes and crawled into the unfamiliar bed, drifting off a few seconds later.

* * * *

Rio tossed the underwear into the hamper and returned to finish the movie he and Ryan had started. "He's in another one of his moods," he grumbled.

Ryan lifted his head and placed it back on Rio's lap. "Cut him some slack. I remember how pissy Quade used to get this time of year."

The long black hair fanning over the edge of the sofa begged for attention. Rio began running his fingers through the thick silk. "If I'd known, I would've put up more of a fight when he wanted to do this mayor crap."

Ryan gazed up into Rio's eyes. "Nate's gratefully shared everything with us since he came into our lives. This is something he wanted for himself. Give him that, will ya?"

His lover always had a way of slapping his hands without coming out and yelling at him. "I just miss him."

"We both do, but we'll get him back after next week. Right now he needs our understanding, not our criticism."

Rio wanted to argue, but knew it would be futile. He returned his attention back to the movie. Life without Nate being, well…Nate, sucked. He hadn't realised how much he depended on his little metrosexual until he wasn't there.

The movie lost its appeal, and Rio turned off the television.

"Hey. I was watching that," Ryan protested, pinching Rio's thigh.

"Sorry. I thought maybe we could go upstairs."

"Okay, but you really coulda asked first." Ryan sat up and swung his legs over the wide leather sofa.

Rio stood and pulled his tattooed man into his arms. "I'm a thoughtless ass sometimes, but you love me anyway."

Ryan nipped Rio's chin. "You're right on both counts."

They turned off the lights and headed upstairs. Walking into their bedroom, Rio was surprised to find the bed empty. "Fuck!"

"Oh, this will not do at all," Ryan growled, turning to stalk out of the room.

Rio followed as Ryan threw open the guestroom door and turned on the light. He threw the covers from Nate's nude body and picked him up. Nate was dead to the world and didn't even stir as he was carried into the master suite.

Working quickly, Rio had the bed turned down and his clothes off in no time. He loved it when Ryan got this way, all commanding and sheriffy.

Ryan laid Nate on the opposite side of the bed and started stripping. "I don't give a shit if he's too tired to fuck, but I'll be damned if I'll have him anywhere but in my bed."

Spread out on his back, with his feet firmly planted on the mattress, Rio let his legs fall open in invitation. "I got what you need right here, Sheriff Blackfeather."

Ryan licked his lips as his hand began to stroke his cock. "You feel like being my prisoner, do ya?"

Wow. How long had it been since Ryan had looked at him with such unbridled lust in his eyes? "Yes. Use me, Lawman. Teach me a lesson."

With a wicked gleam in his eyes, Ryan turned and rifled around in the dresser drawer, finally pulling out a pair of handcuffs. "Turn over."

Rio's eyes went wide. *Kinky motherfucker.* He did as ordered and stretched his arms towards the spindled headboard. The cold metal clicked into place, and Rio started to worry. *What the hell have I gotten myself into?*

He felt the bed dip a second before a large hand slapped him on the ass.

"Ow! What the fuck?" he asked, trying to look over his shoulder.

"Shut up. Prisoners speak when I tell them to speak." A slick finger shoved its way inside Rio's ass. He flinched, not expecting the sudden intrusion.

"Got any contraband in here?" Ryan asked, adding another finger.

"I don't think so, but you might keep looking just in case I forgot something," Rio moaned. He felt the pad of Ryan's finger rub against his prostate and groaned. His cock was soaking the bed sheets with copious amounts of pre-cum. Usually, when Ryan got him this riled up, Nate was there to slurp the dripping liquid into his hot little mouth.

"Fuck me already, Sheriff."

He received a harder slap to his ass. "You want this? I don't think you can handle it. You look like a big candy-assed thug to me."

Rio shoved his ass back as far as he could. "Please fuck me."

Yeah, he was begging, but what the hell. He needed, and needed now.

After another round of Beat-Rio's-Ass, Ryan entered him without his usual gentle nature. Rio almost swallowed his tongue at the sudden invasion. Spots appeared in his line of vision, and he had to take deep breaths to keep from passing out as Ryan assaulted his ass like never before.

Seriously, what the fuck was going on with his Sheriff? Rio began to think Nate's distance of late was affecting Ryan more than he let on.

It was the rough hand pulling on his black curls that finally did it for him. He roared his release as his cock erupted, spraying not only the sheet but his damn pillow as well. *Fuck.*

A sound beside him caught Rio's attention. He turned his head just in time to see Nate come. Rio should probably feel guilty for waking his lover, but from the expression on Nate's sleepy face, his man didn't mind much.

Ryan howled like the Alpha male he was as he thrust deep inside Rio and let loose. Ryan collapsed against Rio's back, and they both fell to the bed below. Now that the excitement had passed, Rio's ass really started to burn. *Damn.* He was going to be sore in the morning.

* * * *

Nate was finishing his first cup of coffee of the day when Ryan walked into the kitchen. "Morning."

Ryan filled a cup with coffee. "Mornin'."

Was it his imagination, or was Ryan pissed about something. "What's wrong?"

His lover leaned a hip against the counter and took a sip of his coffee. "Why'd you go to bed in the guestroom?"

Shit. When he'd woken in bed with Rio and Ryan, he assumed he'd crawled in after the sexy dream he'd had during the night. "Sorry. I was tired."

Ryan slammed his cup onto the counter, hot coffee splashing everywhere. "Let's get something straight. You wanna work yourself 'til all hours of the night, that's your business. But when your fucking job wears you out to the point that you don't end up in my bed at the end of the day, then *we* got problems."

Nate stared at his lover. What the hell? "God forbid I ask for a little fucking support around here. This festival is my first real act as mayor. Forgive me if I wanted to make sure it was done right. I stupidly thought all the long hours I was putting in would end up making you and Rio proud."

He stood, leaving his cup on the table and started to walk out of the kitchen. "I guess I didn't realise my place in this relationship."

Nate hurried his steps. He felt the tears coming, and the last thing he wanted was to cry in front of Ryan. He grabbed up his briefcase and escaped to the more tranquil setting of his convertible.

He heard the front door open and spun out of the drive. *No.* Ryan didn't get a chance to twist what he'd said.

As he drove towards town, Nate tried to push his family problems to the back of his mind. He had so many things yet to do in order for next week's celebration to go off without a hitch.

Once in town, he started to feel better. Friendly faces waved to him as he drove by. He pulled in front of the bakery. Nothing, not even a fight with Ryan, would stop him from his morning cappuccino and maple Long John.

Kyle greeted him as soon as he stepped inside the shop. "Morning, Mayor."

"Morning." Nate got in line behind Naomi, the cute little redhead who owned the bookstore in town. He poked her in the back with his index finger and chuckled at the glare she shot him over her shoulder.

"Watch it, Mister, or I'll report you for harassment."

"Well, if I'm gonna get in trouble for poking you, I might as well grab your ass, too," Nate joked.

Naomi's significant other stepped up and gave Nate the stink eye. "You looking for trouble?"

Nate held up his hands in defence. "Hell, no. Everyone in town knows not to mess with the lesbians. You all could kick my ass."

Naomi laughed. "Gracie Sutherland could kick your butt. It has nothing to do with being a lesbian, jackass."

Nate grinned at the image of little Gracie trying to kick his butt. "Why is it that everyone thinks I'm a wimp? Do I have to remind the residents of this town that not only am I a highly trained private investigator, but I also have several black belts?"

Naomi cocked her head. "Weird how that is, huh?" She shrugged. "I guess you just don't project tough."

"Gee, thanks." Even though he knew Naomi and Courtney were only joking, Nate started to take the banter to heart. They were right. Everyone saw him as the impeccably dressed partner of the two bad asses in town. When did he cease to be seen for what he really was? An impeccably dressed stud who could also kick ass.

Suddenly, coffee didn't sound good. He turned and walked out of Brynn's without a word to anyone. Damn. He hated being in funky moods because they made the day drag on. Not that he had anything to look forward to at home at the end of the night. Well, besides another go 'round with Ryan. He wondered if Rio was as pissy with him as the Sheriff.

Walking into city hall depressed him even further. The air conditioning was acting up again, and it was already hotter than hell in the old mansion turned administrative offices.

"Morning," he told Carol on his way through the outer office.

"Ryan just called."

Nate didn't say a word. He placed his briefcase on his desk and started making a pot of coffee. It felt like he'd only just left the office, and here he was back again.

Carol came bustling in the room and handed him a stack of phone messages. "The people with the portable toilets need you to call them ASAP."

For some reason, that made Nate chuckle. "Perfect. My morning's already gone down the shitter, might as well talk to people who can do something about it."

"Oh, don't start with the sarcasm. Look at this." Carol bent over the desk and stuck the top of her head in his face.

"What? You got dandruff or something?"

"No, idiot, I'm getting grey hair. I've never had that until you came along."

Nate studied his secretary. It was hard for him to tell if the feisty lady was joking or serious. "What're you saying, Carol?"

She put her hands on her curvaceous hips and sighed dramatically. "Why don't you call in the committee heads to deal with some of this stuff? Quade never tried to put Cattle Valley Day's on by himself. It's suicide."

Nate scrubbed his hands over his face. Why didn't anyone understand? "I just want it to be special. I'm putting every ounce of myself into making it that way."

"I know you are, and I'm sure it'll be spectacular, just like you are. But don't forget you do have plenty of people willing and able to help out."

"I know, and I plan to use them to help decorate. Speaking of which, can you get me the phone numbers for the town beautification committee? I know Hearn's, of course, and I'm sure you know George Manning's off the top of your head, but I'll need a full list."

Carol went wide-eyed. "Why would you think I know George's number?"

Nate grinned. "Well, because the two of you worked together for several months, and because I've seen the way you two look at each other."

Carol stood and tossed her hair behind her shoulder. "Flirting's all we do. He's bisexual, and I've had my fill of bisexual men."

Nate leaned back and put his feet on his desk. "Suit yourself, but you'll either have to get over the bisexual thing, or search for a man outside of Cattle Valley."

"Who says I even want a man? I'm perfectly capable of taking care of myself."

"You say it every time you sigh while reading one of those smutty romances you're so fond of."

"They're just books."

"If you say so."

A loud, disgusted grunt came from Carol as she stalked out of his office.

Nate picked up the phone to call the potty people, and it rang, startling him. "Nate Gills."

"Hey, baby. Feel like meeting Ryan and me for lunch later?" Rio asked.

"Not if you're both gonna gang up on me."

"Be nice," Rio admonished.

"Yeah, that's me, Mr. Nice Guy."

"You used to be. I'm not sure what name to call you lately."

Nate bit the inside of his cheek to keep back a smartassed retort. "I've got meetings, but I should be outta here early enough to be home by seven. Guess you'll just have to wait until then to give me an earful."

"What the hell is wrong with you lately? Every time you open your mouth something hateful comes out. Do what you want."

Rio hung up, and Nate was left holding the phone. He shook his head and called the potty people. *Fuck.* He didn't have time to be the happy-go-lucky guy people were used to.

* * * *

Rio spotted Ryan as soon as he entered O'Brien's.

"Pitcher of my usual, please," Ryan told Sean on his way through. He slid into the booth and leaned over to give Rio a kiss. "How's work?"

"Okay." He wouldn't tell Ryan the truth. Sure business was good, but it wasn't the same without Nate there running the place with him. "I got a call from Garron. He wanted to know where they should make hotel reservations."

"Great. So Sonny and Garron are definitely coming for the rodeo?"

"Yep, and everyone else."

Ryan grinned. "I can't wait for Erico to get a look at all those gorgeous Good boys. He'll have to wear a bib while they're in town."

Rio shook his head. "I don't know about that. He's been hot on Jay lately, but Jay won't give him the time of day."

"Good for Jay," Ryan chuckled.

Kitty brought over the pitcher of Coke Ryan had ordered, as well as the big cheeseburgers Rio had pre-ordered. Rio licked his lips. Jay made the best burgers in town. "Thanks, Kitty."

"Enjoy. Let me know if you need anything."

Rio attacked his food. He'd gone without breakfast because of Ryan's mood and Nate's hasty departure. He didn't say anything to his men, but he'd been having a lot of stomach issues lately.

"Damn. You'd better slow down, or you're gonna make yourself sick."

Rio glanced up from his lunch to meet Ryan's gaze. Both of them refused to acknowledge the elephant in the room. Well, actually, the missing elephant in the room. He secretly hoped having their friends from Nebraska visit would pull Nate away from his mayoral duties for a little while.

"So, anything exciting going on around town?" Rio asked.

"Not really. I've spent all morning interviewing guys that've applied to work security for Cattle Valley Days. Most of 'em are Sheridan police officers who're looking for extra cash, but only a few so far are open minded enough to fit in."

"Any cute ones?" Rio asked. He knew Ryan was an extremely jealous lover, and enjoyed keeping him on his toes from time to time.

It worked. Ryan's eyes narrowed over the top of his glass. He set his Coke down and reached across the table. Ryan grabbed a handful of Rio's black curls and pulled him forward until they were nose to nose over the table. "Do you need me to handcuff you to the bed again?"

Memories of the previous night danced wickedly through Rio's mind. Hours later, Rio could still feel Ryan inside of him. "Maybe."

His hand still firmly buried in Rio's hair, Ryan kissed him, tongue thrusting deep. Rio opened wide to receive the openly erotic public display of affection. With a grunt and a grin, Ryan released his hold. "That can be arranged."

They both sat back in their seats and finished their lunch. Rio continued to torture Ryan by slowly licking the ketchup from his fry.

"If I didn't have a meeting with Nate later, I'd take you home right now."

Bringing up Nate's name immediately killed Rio's mood. "Tell him I'm making lasagne for dinner."

Ryan pushed his plate to the centre of the table and sighed. "We had a fight earlier."

"Yeah. I kinda figured that out when I woke up alone in bed and found you in the kitchen growling like a bear."

"He just makes me so damn mad sometimes. Doesn't he realise what he's doing to this relationship?"

Rio felt stomach acid slowly work its way up his oesophagus. Even the mere mention of his relationship being the least bit rocky had Rio wanting to throw up. "I just remembered I have a weight-training class in twenty. I'll have to catch you later at home."

Ryan's head tilted to the side, his long black hair spilling over his shoulder. "You okay? You look a little green."

"I'm fine, just gotta get going." Rio slid out of the booth and gave his lover a quick kiss. "You want me to pay on my way out?"

"Naw, I'll take care of it. Go teach your class."

Rio escaped the pub as quick as he could. He climbed into his truck and turned the air conditioner on full blast. *Please don't throw up.* He needed to hold shit together for another two weeks, and then Nate would be finished working crazy hours, and maybe Ryan would get off his ass.

Two weeks. Rio hoped he wouldn't lose any more weight in that time. According to the scale at *The Gym*, he was already down twelve pounds. It was a wonder his men hadn't noticed, but then again, his men hadn't noticed much other than the tension between the two of them.

Rio put the truck into gear and headed back to work. Despite what he'd told Ryan, he didn't have a class for another two hours, so hopefully he'd get a chance to lie down and get his damn stomach under control.

Chapter Two

After losing the battle to keep his lunch down, Rio gargled with mouthwash and went in search of Mario. He found the martial arts instructor making a fruit smoothie.

"How's it going?" he asked.

"Okay, I guess. Asa called and cancelled another session. Guess he's got to go out of town again." Mario grumbled.

"Damn. That man travels all the time."

"Yeah. Makes it real hard to try and pin him down for a date. Just when I think I've gotten up the nerve to ask him out, he bails on me."

Rio shook his head. Mario and Asa had been dancing around each other for over a year. He wasn't sure what either of them was waiting on. "You just need to tie the sonofabitch down some afternoon during class and ask him."

A devilish expression crossed Mario's face. "Oh, don't think I haven't thought about tying that man down. Although, if I ever succeed, asking for a date will be the last thing on my mind."

Rio choked. He never would've guessed Mario was into the rough stuff. The previous night once again flashed through his mind. "Kinky."

Mario grinned. "Not for a while, but I'm hoping."

"Does Asa have any idea what you're into? Maybe you're scaring him off."

Mario chuckled, flashing his to-die-for dimples. "He hasn't said anything, but I get the feeling he's the kind of man who might enjoy giving up some of that ever-present control once in a while."

Rio laughed right along with Mario. It felt good. So good, in fact, he forgot his plan to lie down. He remembered a time when Nate could make him forget all his worries. Now it seemed Nate and Ryan *were* his worries.

"So, uh, what was that about earlier?" Mario asked, suddenly looking serious.

"What?"

"Tossing your cookies. I notice you've been doing that a lot lately. You're not pregnant, are you?"

Rio was embarrassed that Mario knew his secret. "No. I'm not pregnant. Just been having some trouble with my stomach. Nothing serious."

Mario leaned forward on the juice counter. "That's a load of b.s., and we both know it. So what's going on?"

Rio broke eye contact and glanced around the large, open room. Men and women were working out, either listening to music on their headphones, or watching the big screen televisions he and Nate had strategically placed around the room. So why did *The Gym* seem so empty? *Because Nate's not here.*

"I miss Nate. He doesn't have time for me anymore." Rio shrugged. "Guess I'm letting it get to me."

"Has it been this way since he took over from Quade?"

"Some. Not as bad as it's been lately, though. I keep telling myself that once next weekend is over, I'll get him back, but I don't know anymore. Seems like he's really getting into this mayor thing. After the celebration, I'm sure it'll be something else that needs his attention." *Damn.* He knew he sounded like a girl.

"What's Ryan say about it?"

"Normally he's the one yelling at me for getting upset with Nate, but I guess he and Nate had it out earlier over a cup of coffee."

"And Nate? Has either of you even bothered to actually tell him how you're feeling without it coming out as a challenge?"

How many times had he told his lover he missed him? "Yeah. I've tried. Either he doesn't care, or he's not listening."

He reached down and rubbed his burning stomach. All this talk about Nate had the acid churning again. "Excuse me."

Rio raced to the bathroom and once again threw up. With nothing in his stomach, the only thing to come up was the acid that tasted so vile. He flushed the toilet and poured a small amount of the complimentary mouth wash into a tiny paper cup. He stared at himself in the mirror as he rinsed his mouth. *I don't want to be here.*

He opened the door and almost ran into Mario. The big Italian stood just outside the door with his massive arms crossed over his chest. Mario didn't say a word, but his expression showed his worry.

"I'll be okay. I think I'm gonna head home for the day." Rio didn't wait for an answer, but he got one anyway.

"It won't go away until you deal with it," Mario shouted after him.

* * * *

Ryan stepped inside the Tall Pines ski lodge and strode towards the front desk. "Hey, David, is Chad around?"

"Hi, Sheriff. Something wrong?" David asked, suddenly looking uneasy.

Ryan grinned at the young man. David had run into some trouble in the past, but he'd turned into a damn fine addition to the Cattle Valley community.

"No trouble. Just wanted to catch up with Chad and ask him about some rooms for friends that're coming into town."

"Is there something I can help you with? Chad usually takes a break from twelve to two before The Grizzly Bar starts getting busy."

Ryan tried his best to wipe the knowing smile from his face. He knew exactly what Chad was up to, and he was positive the lodge manager wasn't doing it alone. Ryan glanced at his watch. Chad still had another twenty-five minutes to finish his business with Richard.

"Okay. I'll go ahead and make the reservations and then just wait for Chad in the bar."

David positioned his fingers over the computer keyboard. "What're you looking for in the way of rooms? We're starting to get pretty booked, but I'm sure I can find something."

"I need three rooms. King-sized beds. Close to each other if you got 'em."

David's fingers flew over the keys. "I have a two bedroom suite with a sitting room, and a single room across the hall. I know the suite's more money, but if you factor in the cost of two rooms, it's only a little more."

Ryan nodded. "That'll work. Do they all have king-size beds?"

David glanced at his computer screen. "Yes."

"Good. Go ahead and book 'em for Wednesday through Monday. Put them all under the last name of Good. I'll let the brothers fight it out over who goes where. Do you need a copy of my credit card to hold them?"

"That would probably be best. I know you're good for it, but I'm not always on duty."

Ryan dug out his wallet and handed David his card. Once everything was entered into the computer, Ryan gestured to the bar. "Tell Chad I'd like a word when he gets a chance."

"Will do, Sheriff."

Ryan found a comfortable chair by the wall of windows and settled in. He had a meeting with Nate at three-thirty, and if he was honest with himself, he wasn't looking forward to it.

The thought was like a punch to the gut. Had he ever felt that way? Usually just the sight of the man he loved was enough to set off butterflies in his stomach. Now…what? Ryan wasn't sure. Nate had changed, that much was obvious. It wasn't just since preparations had begun for Cattle Valley Days, either. Something was bothering Nate, but Ryan couldn't seem to get to the root of the problem, no matter how hard he tried.

He spotted Chad and Richard walking towards him.

"Hey," Chad greeted.

"Hey, guys."

"Thought I'd stop by and say hi before heading to the kitchen to make sure all the supplies I ordered came in," Richard said.

"Business good?" Ryan asked.

Richard smiled. "Business is great. We've seen a lot of tourists come in and out. People are taking advantage of the hiking and bike trails."

Ryan nodded. "Yep. I've seen quite a few new faces around town."

Richard shook Ryan's hand and gave Chad a kiss. "I'd better get going."

"I've got friends staying at the lodge for the celebration, so I'm sure you'll see plenty of me."

"Good." Richard waved and retreated to the kitchen.

Chad took a seat beside Ryan, and gazed out over the breathtaking view. "David said you wanted to see me?"

"Yeah. Nothing big, but I wanted to give you a heads-up about the friends coming to town. I'm sure you don't have a problem with it, but among my friends is a threesome made up of twin brothers and their wife. Thought I'd let you know ahead of time so you're not shocked when they check-in."

Chad whistled. "Damn. I've read books, but I've never actually seen..."

"Yeah. It's as hot as you might imagine. Hell, probably hotter," Ryan chuckled.

"Would you like me to tell David? He'll probably be the one checking them in. He's been working double shifts most days to pay off Guy for the damages to the lodge."

"Sure. Don't make a big deal out of it, though. The Good boys are great people. I wouldn't want them embarrassed in any way."

Chad nodded knowingly. "I'll take care of it."

Ryan stood and studied the view once more. "Well, I've got a meeting I'd better get to. See ya around."

"Okay. Let us know if you need anything."

"Will do." Ryan walked out of the bar and headed to his SUV. The butterflies in his stomach had already begun, but they had nothing to do with being anxious to see Nate at their meeting.

* * * *

Leaning back in his chair, Nate watched Ryan's mouth as his lover and George Manning discussed which roads would need to be blocked off for the celebration. A tapping noise drew Nate's attention away from Ryan. It appeared Hearn Sutherland was as bored with the meeting as he was.

Hearn caught Nate staring at him, and laid his pencil down on the conference table. Nate gave him an easy smile, and Hearn smiled back.

He'd been half-hoping Ryan would arrive before the others, so they could clear the air a bit before the meeting, but no such luck. Instead, the tension between them was thick as a San Francisco fog.

Nate watched as Ryan stood and walked over to the large map of Cattle Valley he'd tacked to the wall. He was pointing and explaining how the Sheriff's department would route traffic before the big parade. *Damn, Ryan was sexy.* Nate's gaze travelled from Ryan's strong forearms down his torso to the tight fit of the blue jeans he wore as part of his regular uniform.

"What do you think?"

Nate continued to stare at Ryan's fly, totally oblivious to the fact that all eyes were on him.

Ryan cleared his throat. "Nate. Hello? Are you with us?"

Nate blinked and sat up straight. "I'm sorry. Guess you caught me day-dreamin'."

"I was asking if you'd taken care of getting the school busses to shuttle people into town from the rodeo grounds," Ryan reiterated.

"Uh, yeah. All taken care of. We'll have three busses running continually from the rodeo grounds, and two busses running back and forth from the school parking lot to downtown."

Ryan stared at him for several seconds before turning back to his map. As he started talking about closing roads again, Nate drifted off once more. He was so incredibly tired. Not just physically, but mentally and emotionally. Maybe he needed to get drunk and dance on the tables. Hell. How long had it been since he'd been the life of a party? Too long.

Gone was the fun Nate of yesterday. Mr. Fun was now Mr. Mayor. *What the hell have I gotten myself into?*

The next thing he knew, George stood and gathered his things. Nate's gaze slid to Hearn. "Is it over?" he whispered.

"Finally," he whispered back.

The office emptied in minutes, leaving Nate and Ryan in the room. Nate stood and walked back over to refill his cup. "Care for some more coffee?"

Ryan paused in the process of rolling his map. "Sure."

After refilling his cup, he carried the pot to the table and took care of Ryan's.

"Rio said to tell you he was making lasagne for supper," Ryan mumbled as he slipped a rubber band around the roll of paper.

"Sounds good."

"Good enough for you to actually come home in time to eat it with us?" Ryan asked.

Nate gave Ryan a short nod before slipping behind his desk. If he were a woman, Nate would've sworn he was experiencing PMS. Everything Ryan said had him nearly breaking down in tears.

Ryan brought his coffee over and leaned against the side of Nate's desk. "Sorry about earlier. Guess the hours you're working are starting to get to me."

Get to him? What about all the times Ryan had been forced to fill in for one of his deputies? There'd been weeks when Nate and Rio had barely seen their partner, but they'd both tried to understand. Why was this situation so different?

"It'll be over soon." Nate refused to meet Ryan's penetrating stare. The last thing he wanted was another argument. Silence was better than screaming any day of the week in his opinion.

"Yeah. So you've said." Ryan carried his cup over and set it beside the pot.

Nate clamped his jaw shut in an effort to keep his mouth closed. *Don't say anything. Don't say anything.*

Ryan strode back over and retrieved his map from the table, before coming to a stop beside Nate. "Do I get a kiss before I leave?"

Nate tilted his chin up and gave Ryan a chaste kiss on the lips. "I'll be home for dinner. I promise."

Ryan stared at him for several moments before turning and leaving the office. Nate leaned back in his chair and sighed. Maybe he'd duck out early and stop by O'Brien's. At least Jay always seemed happy to see him.

* * * *

"Hey, Sean."

"Mayor," Sean greeted Nate with a nod.

"Jay busy?"

Sean glanced around the virtually empty bar. "I doubt it. Dinner rush won't start for another thirty minutes or so."

"I won't take up much of his time." Nate entered the kitchen through the swinging door.

"Hey, buddy," he called out.

Jay jumped and spun around, his hand on his chest. "You scared me."

"Sorry." Nate could tell Jay was trying to hide something behind his back. "What've ya got there?"

"Oh, it's nothing. I heard it was Kyle's birthday." Jay glanced over his shoulder and bit his lip. "I'm sure it's not nearly as good as his, but I thought…"

"He'll love it." Nate strode over and gently moved Jay's tiny body out of the way. "Goddamn, Jay. I don't know how the thing tastes, but I do know I've never seen a prettier cake in my life."

Jay tilted his head as he studied the ivory and sage green cake. "You think? I wanted to do something special."

"It's perfect. Really." Nate shook his head. This was exactly the reason he wanted to stop by. No matter what the boy had been through in his life, he always seemed ready to make someone else smile in his own shy way. Nate figured it was Jay's good heart that showed through the emotional scars left by his ex-boyfriend.

"Make sure you let Sean see that before you take it over to Kyle."

"Why?" Jay asked, looking at the floor.

If there was one thing that bothered Nate about Jay, it was his self-defeating personality. Not only did Jay not seem to realise how pretty, or how talented he was, but he rarely looked anyone in the eyes.

Nate reached out and gently lifted Jay's delicate chin until he met his gaze. "It's good. There might be an occasion when Sean could use a cake like that in his catering."

"Oh, I'm not really good enough for something like that. I'm still learning. I bought a book from the clearance rack at Booklovers."

"You learned to do that from a book?" Nate knew of several pastry chefs in Chicago who'd gone to the best culinary schools in the world to learn their trade, and from what he could tell, Jay's cake was every bit as good as one of theirs.

Jay nodded, his head starting to tilt back towards the floor. "I've been practicing at night, but I use cardboard instead of an actual cake."

Nate couldn't help himself. He reached out and pulled the small man into his arms. "You're unbelievable. I'm so glad you came here."

Jay tucked his arms up against his chest and sank into Nate's body, his face turned down. Nate got the distinct impression Jay needed this. It wasn't a sexual hug by any stretch of the imagination. More like the kind of hug a parent would give a child. He couldn't help but wonder if Jay's parents had ever held him.

Nate kissed the top of Jay's hair. "You smell good."

Jay laughed, the sound like musical notes working their way up and down a scale. "I spilled amaretto extract on myself."

"Well, it's nice whatever it is." He finally released Jay and took a step back. "I need to get home for dinner, and you need to get that cake finished before you have to start flipping burgers."

"Yeah," Jay replied in that mesmerising voice Nate loved.

"Save me a dance next Saturday night."

Jay shook his head. "I won't be at the dance. I'm babysitting Gracie and Joey."

"Well, maybe I'll send Ryan up to give you a break for a few minutes. You have to dance at least once. I've worked really hard to make this the best party Cattle Valley has ever seen. I'd be hurt if you didn't show up."

Jay's expression turned worried. "I don't know how to dance."

"Bullshit. I've seen you dancin' babies around a room. You've got the moves. You just haven't tried them on anyone old enough to really wrap you in their arms. It's a feeling like none other."

Jay grinned. "Okay."

"Good. I'm looking forward to it."

Nate left O'Brien's with a smile on his face.

He arrived home at six on the dot and let himself inside. "I'm home," he called out.

Rio appeared in the kitchen doorway. "You made it. I was just getting ready to put the garlic bread in the oven."

There was something so wholesome in the way the big man gazed at him. Despite the tension between the three of late, Nate needed his men. He strode towards Rio, hoping he'd be welcomed in those strong arms. His wish was granted when Rio opened to him. Nate immediately wrapped his arms around his lover.

He knew Rio and Ryan thought otherwise, but he really did miss them. The job he'd been elected to do wasn't what he'd expected at all. For some reason he'd thought it would be a good chance to really get to know people in the community. Instead, he was usually stuck behind a desk under a pile of papers.

Rio's hands felt good rubbing up and down his back. Nate moulded himself further against his partner. "I love you," he whispered before giving Rio a kiss.

Damn Rio tastes good. How long had it been since he'd indulged in the flavours of his men?

A sigh from Rio caught Nate's attention. It wasn't the sound of lust or love. Nate pulled back and looked into Rio's eyes. "Something wrong?"

Rio shook his head. "I needed to hear that, is all."

Nate cupped Rio's gorgeous face and kissed his chin. "You know even though I don't always find the time to say it, I always feel it."

A build-up of moisture in Rio's eyes nearly broke Nate's heart. "You do know that, right?"

He watched Rio's Adam's apple bob several times before he spoke. "I've missed you so much."

The simple sentence had Nate on the verge of tears. What the hell was he doing to his family?

The front door slamming shut sounded Ryan's arrival. Nate stayed where he was, tucked safely in Rio's embrace. He felt Ryan step up behind him, pressing that strong body against him.

There was absolutely nothing in the world like the feeling of being sandwiched between the two men he loved. Ryan bent and kissed Nate's neck. Nate tilted his head to the side to give Ryan more room. When the kissing didn't resume, he glanced over his shoulder.

Ryan's eyes were narrowed. *Uh oh.* Nate knew the look well. Hell, he should, he'd been on the receiving end quite a bit lately. "What's wrong?"

"What's that smell?"

Nate tried to figure out what Ryan was talking about. He knew he'd put on deodorant. *Shit.* "Does it smell like Amaretto?"

Ryan took a step back and spun Nate around to face him. "How the hell should I know what Amaretto smells like? All I know is you don't smell like Nate. You smell like someone else."

Nate nodded. "Jay. I stopped by O'Brien's on my way home to see how he was doing."

"And what? You felt the need to get up close and personal with him?"

For fuck's sake. It seemed like every time he turned around lately he was getting yelled at for something. "It's Jay. And yeah, I felt the need to give him a hug. Since when are you so fucking paranoid?"

"Since you decided to sleep somewhere other than my bed," Ryan growled.

Nate squared his shoulders and held a finger in front of Ryan's face. "One night. One. I was so goddamned tired I couldn't see straight. Forgive me for not being your fuck toy for one goddamned night."

A crash from the kitchen stopped the fight dead. Nate and Ryan both ran to investigate. Nate was ashamed he hadn't even noticed Rio's absence. They found the back door open and the glass dish of lasagne smashed on the floor.

Shit. Rio's truck spraying gravel as it sped out of the driveway was the only sound they heard. "I'll go after him."

Ryan grabbed Nate's upper arm. "No you won't. I'll go."

"Seriously? Now you want to fight about this? Why the hell do you think he left in the first place? We were enjoying a beautiful moment when you barged in and started chewing my ass for something as innocent as giving Jay a hug."

"It wasn't about the hug," Ryan mumbled.

Nate wrapped his arms around himself. "What's happening to us?"

Despite the question, Nate already knew the answer. The trouble started when he'd become mayor. "Do you want me to resign?"

Ryan shook his head. "I just want my family back."

"So tell me how to do that. Seriously, I need you to tell me, because I have no clue how to be all things to everybody and still have a tiny bit left for myself."

Ryan's voice softened even further. "You start by letting the people who love you, help you. There's no shame in accepting help from others, Nate. You've got an entire town of people who'd do anything you asked of them. Why is it so important for you to shut everyone out?"

Nate bit his tongue. His men had worked so hard to get him elected. There was simply no way he could tell Ryan the truth. Maybe if he let Rio and Ryan help him things could go back to normal. "Okay. But first I need to go find Rio and talk to him."

"Would you mind if I went with you?" Ryan asked.

Nate shook his head. "I think that would go a long way in getting him to come back home."

Chapter Three

Rio wasn't sure how long he drove around before finally heading towards Mario's place. He knew Ryan and Nate were probably out looking for him, but Rio wasn't ready to be found.

The tiny house Mario rented was dark when he pulled into the drive. He almost left again, but spotted a flicker of light behind the front curtains. With a deep breath, Rio climbed out of the pickup. He knocked on Mario's door and waited. *I probably should've called.*

"Hang on," Mario yelled from inside.

When Mario opened the door, Rio almost swallowed his tongue. There, in front of him, stood a Mario he'd never seen. "You going out?"

Mario glanced down at his skin-tight black leather pants and shook his head. "Nope," he chuckled.

"Someone coming in?"

Mario laughed harder. "No. This is what I feel most comfortable in when I'm at home."

Rio ran a hand through his hair. He felt a little uncomfortable knowing this side of his friend. Why the hell was he finding all this out now? "How long have we been friends?"

"I don't know, a year and a half or so, why?"

"Exactly. Why didn't I know you were one of those leather guys?"

With an amused expression, Mario stepped back and gestured for Rio to enter. "Want something to drink?"

"I could use a beer if you have one," Rio answered as he glanced around the small living room. He saw that a movie had been paused, a close-up of a man's face frozen in time on the screen. Rio wondered if Mario was watching a BDSM porno or something.

Curiosity got the better of him, and he picked up the DVD jacket from on top of the television. *Much Ado About Nothing?*

"Surprised?" Mario asked. He handed Rio a beer and took a seat on the couch.

"Yeah, actually. I didn't know you liked Shakespeare."

Mario tilted his head to the side. "It appears there's a lot about me that you don't know. I like Shakespeare, leather, and fucking a man so hard it makes his teeth rattle. But you didn't come here to find out about me. What's going on?"

Rio couldn't get the image of Mario fucking out of his mind. *Damn.*

"Rio?"

Rio shook his head and took a drink of his beer. "Had to get out of the house. Ryan and Nate were at each other's throats again."

It was uncharacteristic for Rio to expose his feelings so openly, but he needed to talk to someone, and from what he could see, Mario was good at keeping secrets. "I grew up with that, ya know. I couldn't deal with it then, and I can't deal with it now."

Mario's hand reached across the back of the couch and wound its way into Rio's black curls. "You and I both know you're giving yourself an ulcer. Do you want it to turn into a serious problem like Casey's did?"

"No, but I can't tell my body to ignore my mind. If I'm worried, I'm worried."

Mario absently scratched the back of Rio's head. "What're you worried about exactly?"

Rio swallowed around the lump in his throat. Memories of a thirteen-year-old boy sitting in front of a judge, assaulted him. *Who would you like to live with, Rio?* What no one had bothered to tell him was that the choice he made would forever change his life.

"If things don't work out between Ryan and Nate, I won't choose between them," Rio answered vehemently. Just the idea of being put into that position again had Rio grabbing his stomach. "Can I use your bathroom?"

Mario nodded and pointed. "First door on the left."

* * * *

"Hey, Sean, you haven't seen Rio in here have you?"

"Not since lunch. Is there something wrong?" Sean asked.

Ryan waved away his friend's apparent concern. "Nothing we can't handle. Thanks."

He left the bar and climbed back into the SUV. "Sean hasn't seen him."

"Well, shit."

Ryan's cell phone erupted with Indian Outlaw by Tim McGraw. "Maybe that's him," he said as he pulled his phone out.

"Rio?"

"Nope, but I know where he is," Mario answered.

"We'll be right there."

"If you and Nate are still acting like a couple of jackasses, don't bother. I just thought I'd let you know he was safe."

What could he say to that? He knew Mario was right. They had been acting like a couple of children. "We're working on it. We'll be there in five minutes."

Ryan hung up and tossed the phone to the console between them. "He's at Mario's."

Nate placed a hand on Ryan's thigh. "You think we'll be able to get him to come home with us?"

Ryan's chest ached. That was the first time in days Nate had voluntarily touched him. He covered his lover's hand with his own and squeezed. "All we can do is try and assure him that we're gonna work together from now on."

Nate nodded and turned to stare out the passenger window, but he left his hand on Ryan's leg. One step at a time, Ryan told himself.

Ryan parked in front of Mario's house and turned off the engine. He lifted Nate's hand and kissed it. "Ready to do some damage control?"

"I just hope he gives us the chance," Nate mumbled. He pulled his hand away and got out of the SUV before Ryan could say anything further.

Ryan met up with his lover on the sidewalk and pulled him into his arms. Nate's body felt stiff, but Ryan wasn't about to release him. "I can't imagine my life without you. You're the sunshine in my day."

Nate's body relaxed against his. "I love you, too."

Ryan bent and covered Nate's mouth with his own, slipping his tongue between his partner's lips.

* * * *

Embarrassed, Rio stepped out of the bathroom. "I hope you don't mind, I borrowed some of your toothpaste."

Mario was straddling the arm of the sofa. Rio knew if he wasn't hopelessly in love with Ryan and Nate, he'd be trying his best to get into those skin-tight leather pants. Why was he just now noticing how sexy Mario was? He always knew the guy was a stud, but the more he got to know him, the hotter Mario became. Mario's earlier statement about fucking a man hard enough to rattle teeth had goosebumps breaking out on Rio's skin.

Headlights stopping in front of the house drew Rio's attention. He glanced at his friend. "Did you call 'em?"

Mario nodded. "I told them not to come unless they'd stopped acting like a couple of jackasses. Didn't want them to worry though."

Rio stepped up to the window in the still darkened room, and peered out. He was shocked by the silhouette of his lovers kissing. Rio's cock hardened even further. He turned back to Mario. "I'd better go with them."

Crossing his arms, Mario nodded but said nothing.

Before moving towards the door, Rio stepped up to his friend. He cupped the side of Mario's face and gave him a chaste kiss on the lips. "Thank you. Your time will come."

"From your lips to God's ears," Mario said. Despite the smile, Rio could see the loneliness in Mario's dark eyes.

Rio pulled away and walked out the front door. He didn't wait for an invitation to join his men. Instead, he strode up to them and wrapped Nate and Ryan in his arms. Nate and Ryan broke their kiss and turned towards Rio.

"We're so sorry," Nate apologised between kisses.

"Have you guys made up?" Rio asked.

Nate looked at Ryan and nodded. "Can we take you home?"

"You make me sound like a puppy."

Nate chuckled and slipped his hand under Rio's T-shirt. "You can be my puppy, if I can rub your belly."

Rio smiled. The twinkle in Nate's eyes had been missing for so long that Rio had forgotten what it did to his insides. "I'll follow you home."

Nate pulled Rio's head down for a kiss before whispering in his ear. "I'm going to ride home with Ryan. Things are better, and I'd like to keep it that way. Too much time to think and you know how he gets."

Rio nodded his understanding and released his lover.

Nate tugged on Rio's hair, pulling him back down again. "Why do you taste like toothpaste?"

Rio felt his face heat. "I threw up and borrowed some of Mario's."

"You threw up?" Ryan asked, turning Rio more fully towards him. "Are you sick?"

Rio shook his head. "I just got upset. I'm okay now."

Ryan's gaze shot from Nate back to Rio. "We'll see you at home."

Nate was herded towards the SUV in typical Ryan fashion. If nothing else, at least his two men were acting more like their old selves. He hopped into his truck and fired up the engine. He noticed a shadow at Mario's front window and waved as he pulled out of the drive.

* * * *

Nate sat in the chair beside the bed and watched his men sleep. How long had he been sitting there? He glanced at the clock and determined he'd only had about two hours sleep. He'd need to get into the shower in thirty minutes.

He rubbed his eyes and wondered if mayors were allowed to call in sick the week before a huge celebration. Nate watched as Rio's hands reached out for him in sleep. When they met Ryan's much bigger body, his eyes popped open.

"I'm over here," Nate whispered.

Rio looked over the top of Ryan. "What're you doing over there, baby?"

Hugging his legs to his chest, Nate shrugged. "Couldn't sleep."

"Come back to bed."

Nate stood and walked around the end of the bed. He climbed over a delightfully naked Rio and landed in the usual spot. Within seconds, he was wrapped in his lover's warm embrace.

"Why can't you sleep?" Ryan asked, spooning against Nate's back.

"I don't know. Every time I close my eyes, I have nightmares about bulls getting out of the pen and stampeding, or Trick Allen's bus breaking down on the way to the dance." He shrugged again. "It's always something different."

Rio tilted Nate's chin up. "You're not God. You may think you are at times, but you're not. You're worrying about things you have no control over."

"Well, to be honest, I also worry about things I do have control over."

"What's really bothering you?"

Rio was studying him so intently Nate didn't know what to say.

"Haven't you learned nothing good comes from keeping secrets?" Rio asked.

"You're one to talk. How many times in the last month have you thrown up, and don't lie!"

"A couple," Rio mumbled.

"A couple? Are you sure?" Ryan questioned Rio further.

"Maybe a little more," Rio confessed.

"Should we make you an appointment at the clinic?" Nate asked.

"Naw. I'll be fine as long as we're all okay."

Ryan reached across Nate and pulled Rio closer. "Arguing with the people you love most in the world sucks, but you can't let it affect your health."

"It's not like I throw up on purpose."

Nate was ashamed of himself, but he much preferred the focus being on Rio instead of him. "Have you always been that way?" he asked.

"No. I used to go out, track and kill bad guys when I got upset. Unfortunately, that option is no longer available."

Nate thought of the years Rio spent as a mercenary in Mexico and South America. He was thankful his lover no longer pursued that particular career. He realised he'd never really asked about Rio's life before they got together. He knew Rio didn't like talking about his years in the jungles of the world, so he'd always shied away from bringing up the past.

"How old were you when you became a mercenary?" he finally asked.

"Twenty-six or thereabouts. I joined the Marines when I was seventeen, the day after I graduated. I liked the work, but had trouble with a few of their rules."

"Don't ask, don't tell?" Nate guessed.

"Yeah, that was the big one. But I also decided I wasn't meant to follow orders that didn't always make sense to me."

"What about before that?" Nate asked.

"Before what?"

"Before you joined the Marines." The only thing Nate knew about Rio's childhood was that his mother had died when he was barely in his teens. He'd asked several times, but Rio always seemed to change the subject before divulging any real information. Rio always said his life started the day he became a Marine.

Rio rolled over on top of Nate and kissed him. Nate knew it was Rio's way of shutting him up, but he'd divulged a lot for him, so Nate decided to give the man a break. He wrapped his legs around Rio's waist and ate hungrily at his lover's mouth.

Rio drew his legs up and broke the kiss. "You gonna let me in this ass?" Rio asked, prodding Nate's hole with the tip of his cock.

Nate was about to ask Ryan for the bottle of lube when slick fingers began working his hole. "Fuck, that feels good."

The previous night had been about making Rio feel loved, but now. *Oh, damn.* Now he wanted to feel Rio's thick meat push inside of him. Nate closed his eyes and pushed against Ryan's fingers as they worked their magic inside his ass.

"You want daddy to fuck you hard enough to make your teeth rattle," Rio growled.

Nate's eyes sprung wide open. "What?"

Rio grinned. "Something I heard recently."

Nate shook his head. "I don't think I want to know where."

"Probably not," Rio agreed. "Get them fingers outta there, Ryan, cuz I'm going in."

Nate chuckled as Rio slapped at Ryan's hand. God, it felt good to laugh. His old fashioned alarm clock went off, and Nate reached out, snagged the damn thing, and threw it across the room. They all started laughing when the clock broke into large pieces but continued to ring.

"Time for you to go digital, baby," Ryan remarked.

"Whatever. Forget the clock and think about the cock. In. My. Ass."

Rio quickly poured a few drops of lube onto his shaft and positioned the crown just inside Nate's hole. Before thrusting forward he regarded Ryan. "What part you feel like playing in this? You wanna fuck my ass or Nate's mouth?"

Ryan reached behind Rio and grunted. "Feels like you're pretty sore back there. I'll take it easy on you and feed Nate his breakfast."

Nate rolled his eyes. He hated when his men discussed him without consulting him. "Who says I want your seed for breakfast? Maybe I was hoping for waffles."

Rio thrust forward in one smooth move.

Any protest he might've given flew out the window. Nate opened his mouth for Ryan's pre-cum dripping cock. "Feed me."

* * * *

"Ooh, someone got laid this morning," Carol noted when Nate finally strolled into the office.

"What was your first clue? The fact that I'm two hours late, or that I can't seem to walk without looking like a damn cowboy?"

"Giddy up," she chuckled.

Nate couldn't wipe the smile from his face as he walked to the coffee pot. "Hey, Carol, would you call Hearn for me and see if he can come in?"

"Sure enough, cowboy."

Rolling his eyes, he carried his coffee to the desk and sat down gingerly.

"Hearn'll be here as soon as he drops Gracie at the flower shop," Carol yelled.

"Thanks."

After a long talk with his men the previous night, Nate decided to ask for help. As much as he loved his pride, he loved his men more, and he knew things couldn't continue like they had been.

Strangely enough, the one person he knew he could go to for help was the very man who had wanted his job in the first place. But Nate knew Hearn didn't hold a grudge about losing the election.

In fact, Hearn had confided in him that he'd decided to run more for Tyler's sake than his own. With the addition of his new duties as Parks and Recreation Director, Hearn was happier than he'd ever been.

The phone rang. "I'll get it," he called.

"Be my guest."

"Nate," he answered.

"Hey, it's Rance. I've got some bad news."

Nate closed his eyes and leaned his head against the back of his chair. *Shit*. There went his good mood. Bad news from the outfit providing rodeo stock wasn't something he'd been prepared to hear.

"Whatcha got?" he finally asked.

"I don't know if it's too late to change the programmes for the rodeo, but the boss just shot Zero Tolerance."

"Jesus! What happened? He go after Bo again?"

"Worse. He went after Bo while he was carrying Joey. And I think we both know how protective Shep is of that baby. I don't know if I've ever seen him so het up."

"Are they okay?" Nate didn't even want to think about a bull of that size going after an infant.

"They're fine. Joey never even woke up."

"Good." Nate breathed a sigh of relief. "I'll ask Carol to check on the programmes. You have an alternative?" Nate was busy thanking the big man upstairs, when Hearn walked into the office.

"We're gonna try out one of our newest acquisitions, Satan's Bandit."

"Oh hell. I'm glad I'm not riding."

Rance chuckled. "I'm not sure how he'll be in the arena, but he's not half as bad as Zero was here on the ranch."

Nate knew it wasn't any of his business, but he had to know. "Is Bo breathing easier since Shep put Zero down?"

"That's the hell of it. Bo seemed more upset than anyone. If I live to be a hundred, I'll never understand the twisted relationship those two had."

"I hear ya. Well, Hearn's here, so I'd better get off the phone. Tell Shep the change is fine."

"Will do. Thanks, Nate."

Nate hung up the phone, still chuckling. "Shep shot old Zero Tolerance for looking cross-eyed at baby Joey."

Hearn whistled. It didn't take a genius to know just how much money Shep had just cost himself. All rodeo bulls had high dollar insurance, but no company in their right mind would pay out on a death like that.

"Would you like a cup of coffee?" Nate asked as he got up to refill his.

"No thanks. Tyler has me on two cups a day, and I've already met my quota."

"I wanted to know if you had time in your schedule to help me get things together for the dance. I think I have most everything ordered, but I have quite a few things picked up from Sheridan, and I'm in desperate need of volunteers to help decorate."

"Sure. I've told you all along I'd do anything I could to help."

"I know you did. I'm sorry it took so long for me to get my head outta my ass."

"Tyler told me this morning the new hanging baskets you ordered for all the light poles on Main Street will be delivered by Friday. I can contact the Beautification Committee and ask for volunteers to help hang them."

"That'd be fantastic. What about the flowers for the new planters? Will they be here Friday as well?"

"I'm not sure, but I'll find out."

Nate nodded. "I've got that big outfit coming in from Casper to set up the stage, but they can't do that until the day of, because Main Street will have to be closed."

Nate continued to run through the list in his head. "Oh, the beer garden. It took a lot of sweet talk, but I managed to get Erico and Sean to work together this year, so hopefully the garden will resemble an outdoor lounge instead of just tables and hay bales stuck behind a rope strung between trees."

With his hands clasped and resting on his chest, Hearn grinned.

"What?"

"It's obvious why you've been so grouchy lately. I know everyone will notice and appreciate the changes you're making, but you know it wasn't necessary, right?"

Although he knew Hearn didn't mean it as a reprimand, that's what it felt like. He'd worked damn hard trying to make this the best Cattle Valley Days ever, what was so wrong with that?

"We both know I don't do anything half-assed," Nate replied. He played the comment off like it didn't bother him.

"Ain't that the truth," Hearn chuckled.

Nate couldn't help but wonder whether or not he'd made a mistake by asking for help. Would the townspeople treat him as a joke? He simply wanted to give them the best Cattle Valley Days the town had ever seen. Maybe Hearn was right. Maybe he was going over the top?

"Is there anything else?" Hearn asked.

"Uh, no, not that I can think of. If you'll call your volunteers and ask them about the hanging baskets and getting the flowers into the planters, we should be good until the day of the dance."

Hearn nodded and stood. "I'll take care of it. By the way, we have eight teams signed up for the baseball tournament."

"Excellent. I'm sure I'll show up to at least one of Ryan and Rio's games."

"Too bad you couldn't play this year," Hearn said on his way to the door.

"Yeah, well, too many irons in the fire this year."

He gave Hearn a parting wave and picked up a file like he had work to do. Well, he did have work to do, but his mind wasn't on it. He waited a few minutes before venturing into Carol's office.

"Do I have any appointments?"

Carol looked at the calendar on her desk. "Nope."

"Good. I'm going out for a while. If anyone needs me, call me on my cell." He started out the door, but stopped and turned back. "Shit. I almost forgot. Can you call the printer and see if it's too late to change the programme for the rodeo? Zero Tolerance is out and Satan's Bandit's in."

"Wow. You going to tell me why, or just leave me hanging?"

Nate winked and opened the door. "I'll tell you when I get back. That way I know you'll still be here."

"Wrong, Mr. Smarty Pants. I have a dial finger, and I'm not afraid to use it."

Nate chuckled. Carol was as much of a busybody as he was. It was probably why the two of them got along so well. "Have fun."

Chapter Four

Rio closed his phone and slipped it into his pocket. "Nate's running typically late, but he'll be here."

Ryan nodded and sipped at his drink. "Hopefully, he'll get here before everyone else does."

Their friends from Nebraska had arrived at Tall Pines two hours earlier, but had begged a shower before the planned barbeque. Rio opened the refrigerator and put away the fruit salad he'd just made.

With his hands on his hips, he tried to determine if everything was ready. Usually, Nate was the host for these kinds of get-togethers, but with all the last minute preparations for the celebration, it had been left up to him and Ryan.

Rio glanced at his lover, kicked back in one of the more comfortable chairs in the kitchen. *So much for a team effort.* He shook his head, and started getting out the plates and glasses. The easiest thing would've been to go with paper plates and plastic glasses, but Rio knew Nate would die if he served guests that way.

The sound of crunching gravel signalled an arrival. Rio looked out the kitchen window. "They're here," he announced as he took off the simple white baker's apron.

Ryan swung his legs down from the chair they'd been resting on and stood. Rio grabbed his hand and pulled him towards the front door. They stood on the porch as seven gorgeous adults climbed out of the big black Suburban.

Rawley and Jeb were the first to reach them.

"Hey, strangers," Rio greeted as he shook hands with the two men.

When Garron walked up the porch steps, he knocked Rio's hand away and pulled him into a hug. "Missed you guys."

"We've missed you, too," Rio replied. He let go of Garron and pulled Sonny into his arms. "How's life living with a lawman?"

"You should know," Sonny chuckled.

"You have my sympathy."

Sonny stepped back and the twins, Ryker and Ranger made their way onto the porch with their wife, Lilly tucked between them.

Although Rio didn't know Lilly well, he hugged her anyway. "Nice of you all to come. I'm sure you're worn out from the drive."

Lilly let out a giggle. "I think Garron and I were the only ones awake for most of the trip. You get these Good boys into a car, and it's like they've taken a sleeping pill."

"At least we'll be wide awake later," Ranger said with a wink.

Lilly rolled her eyes and the group headed into the house.

"So where's the pretty one?" Garron asked as they made their way out to the patio.

"Nate had a few last minute things to take care of. He should be here any minute." A horn sounded as soon as the words left Rio's mouth. "Speak of the devil."

"Things going any better for him?" Garron asked.

Rio could tell by the expression on the man's face that he'd obviously talked to Nate at some point since he'd taken over as mayor. There was something in the way Garron asked that had Rio's hackles up. Did Garron know something he didn't?

"He's finally asking for help, but he still takes too much of it on himself. We'll see how things go after the celebration is over."

Garron was the first to reach Nate when he stepped onto the patio, grabbing Rio's Nate up into a bear hug. Although Rio knew Nate and Garron had known each other for years, he was man enough to acknowledge the streak of jealousy that raced through him.

Nate was unceremoniously passed from person to person until all greetings were out of the way. Nate started to sit in the chair beside him, but Rio needed his lover closer. He pulled Nate into his lap and gave him a quick kiss.

"I'm happy you're home," he whispered in Nate's ear.

"I'm happy to be home." Nate gazed up at Rio with those beautiful light brown eyes.

Uh oh, his little man wanted something. "What?"

"Elliott Simms called me on the way home. He was supposed to take tickets at the rodeo on Saturday, but he threw his back out stocking dog food at the grocery store."

"And?"

"I was wondering if I could talk you into doing it?"

"Will I still be able to see the rodeo from where I'll be standing?"

"Yes. And with your height, you shouldn't have any trouble seeing over someone if they get in your way."

Taking tickets all day in the sun wasn't Rio's idea of a good time, but he knew Nate wouldn't have asked unless he really needed him. "Sure. Just tell me when to show up, and I'll be there."

"You're the best," Nate said before giving Rio's mouth a slow and sexy tongue fuck.

Ryan cleared his throat, reminding Rio they weren't alone. He knew it was nothing their friends hadn't seen before, but he'd already promised Ryan he'd be on his best behaviour.

"So the parade is Saturday morning, and then the rodeo, right?" Ryker asked.

"Yeah, but the preliminaries for the rodeo are all day tomorrow. Then the finals on Saturday. Then after that comes the big street dance," Nate informed the group.

"What else is going on tomorrow besides the rodeo?" Jeb asked.

"Well, the carnival will be running both days, but then there's the bake-offs, cook-offs, baseball tournament..." Nate stopped. "Oh, shit."

"What?" Rio asked as he rubbed Nate's back.

"I forgot about you and Ryan playing in the baseball tournament. What if you make it to the finals on Saturday?"

Ryan shook his head. "Don't you remember? You had the finals changed to Sunday so they wouldn't interfere with the parade?"

Nate sighed and leaned back against Rio's chest. "I swear I'm losing my mind."

Snuggled up against him, Rio felt the vibrations of Nate's stomach growling. "Is that my cue to start the grill?"

"Would you mind? I haven't eaten all day."

"Nope. Let me up, and I'll get started." Rio gave Nate's ass a playful slap as he stood.

"Why don't you show me the horses I keep hearing so much about?" Garron asked Nate.

"Sure," Nate agreed and took off towards the barn with Garron following.

Rio stopped just inside the door and watched the two men heading across the field. He wished he knew what they were talking about.

* * * *

Nate turned on the light in the barn as they entered. The sound of the fans blowing made it hard to talk, but he was glad to get Garron alone. His old friend was the only person he'd confided his fears in.

"Now. Tell me the truth as to how things are going."

Nate sat on a bale of hay and gazed up at his friend. "Well, the planning is going a lot smoother since I started asking for help, but what do I do next week?"

"You get up and go to work."

"Easy for you to say. You know how to be a sheriff. I know nothing about being a mayor. You know me, if it was up to me, every city employee would get a big raise every year. But now I'm in the position where I have to kinda pick and choose, and that's just not me."

Nate started to run his fingers through his hair, but thought better of it. He was having a damn good hair day, so why mess with perfection? "And it's not just the raises. It's everything. I'm so afraid I'm going to do something wrong, I'm afraid to do *anything*."

"I think you need to relax and cut yourself some slack. Everyone knows you're new to the job. I doubt they expect perfection. Besides, they voted for you, they must believe in you."

Nate buried his face in his hands. That was exactly the problem. "They voted for me because they like me, not because I was more qualified for the job than Hearn. It was nothing more than a popularity contest. Well, now I've been crowned homecoming king, but I don't know what the hell to do with the crown."

"Weren't you friends with the old mayor?"

"Quade? Sure, but he's off living a life most of us only dream about. He doesn't have time to hold my hand."

"How do you know, have you asked him?"

"No."

"It might not be a bad idea. Hell, the guy might even be flattered. But you sittin' around beating yourself up over it on a daily basis isn't going to get the job done."

"You're right." Nate sighed. "I miss the days of hanging out at *The Gym* with Rio."

"Now you're starting to sound like a spoiled brat. You've taken an oath to serve this town. It's your duty as a man and a member of the community to fulfil your term."

Why did Nate suddenly feel like he was sitting in front of his high school principal? Because Garron was right, he was acting like a brat. "I'll call Quade next week and see if he can offer a few suggestions," he relented.

Garron clapped Nate on the back, nearly sending him to the dirt floor. "Good man."

Nate stood and dusted off the seat of his pants. "Let me introduce you to our babies while we're out here just in case Rio quizzes you at dinner."

* * * *

After dinner Ryan suggested they all go to the Grizzly Bar for a drink. Nate was so tired he could barely keep his eyes open, but when he'd tried to get out of going, Ryan had called him out. He said their friends had come into town and spending time with them was worth a few hours of lost sleep.

Nate didn't want to upset Rio in any way by arguing the point with Ryan, so he reluctantly agreed. He felt Rio's hand land on his thigh and smiled.

"You doing okay?" Rio whispered in his ear.

Nate nodded. "A little tired, but I'm fine."

Rio's gorgeous face tilted to the side. "You sure, baby? Cuz you've got dark circles under your eyes."

The last thing Nate wanted to hear was that his looks were suffering. He glanced at Ryan who was telling a story. He didn't begrudge his lover an evening with their friends. Hell, Nate wished he felt like drinking and having a good time, but it just wasn't happening.

He continued to receive suspicious glances from Garron throughout the evening. Nate hoped Rio didn't notice. Although he loved his big mercenary dearly, Rio could read things into a situation that wasn't there, and lord knew the man was a jealous lover.

A yawn came out of nowhere that he couldn't hide. *Shit.*

"Time to get you home," Rio said. He gave Nate several gentle kisses before waving Ryan over.

Ryan stopped mid-story and strode towards them. "What's up?"

"We need to get Nate home. The poor little feller can barely keep his eyes open."

Ryan glanced around the table and finally nodded. "Okay. Let's say goodbye and get going."

Nate gave his friends hugs goodbye, explaining he'd see them all downtown the following morning.

When it became Garron's turn, his friend held him close and whispered in his ear. "Talk to your men. Rio's been giving me the stink eye all evening."

Nate nodded and stepped back. He turned towards Rio and held out his hand. Rio led him to the door and into the Tall Pines lobby. They waited for several moments, but Ryan didn't appear.

"I'll go prod him in the ass," Rio growled.

Nate took a seat in one of the comfortable leather wingback chairs and waited. He struggled to keep his eyes open, but eventually lost the battle.

"Wake up, baby."

Nate opened his eyes when he felt strong arms lift him from the chair. "Sorry," he mumbled, snuggling in against Rio's chest.

"Not your fault."

Nate may have been damn near asleep again, but he heard the anger in the gentle giant's voice. *Uh oh.*

"I can walk." Nate tried to swing his legs down, but Rio caught him back up.

"You stay where you are. I'll take care of you."

"Was that a dig at me?" Ryan asked.

"Yeah, I guess it was. I told you damn near forty minutes ago it was time to get out of here," Rio barked.

"Lilly wanted to show me the wedding pictures. What was I supposed to do?" Ryan asked.

Although awake, Nate kept his eyes closed. This was one argument he wanted no part in. He heard the truck door open a second before he was deposited in the centre of the bench seat.

The door slammed, and Rio buckled him in and pulled him against his side. "Just rest your head on my shoulder."

"Don't argue," he whispered in Rio's ear.

Rio tried his best to smile. "Okay, baby."

The driver's door opened and Ryan climbed in. Before starting the pickup, he reached over and cupped Nate's cheek. "I'm sorry. I guess I was having fun, and I just...sorry."

"There's nothing wrong with having fun. If you want to take me home and come back, that's fine with me."

"We've all got a long weekend ahead of us. I was caught up in the moment, but there'll be others." Ryan removed his hand and started the truck.

The drive down the mountain seemed shorter than usual. Had he fallen asleep again? Although Ryan and Rio wrapped arms around him, Nate insisted on walking into the house on his own two feet.

His lovers helped him undress and before he knew it, he was sound asleep sandwiched between Rio and Ryan's gorgeous bodies.

* * * *

Nate walked down Main Street, amazed at what he saw, or what he didn't see. Where was everyone? Cattle Valley looked like a ghost town. The over-flowing baskets that had been hung the previous week were either on the ground or dried up still hanging on the light poles.

He spotted Jay coming out of the door that led up to his apartment and rushed over. "Where is everyone?"

Jay sneered at him and jumped back. "They went to the carnival up in Sheridan."

"What? Why? We're supposed to be having a celebration right here."

Jay snorted. "Yeah. A lame celebration. It was so much better when Quade was in charge. We've seen the way you've been running around like a chicken with its head cut off. No way we wanted to trust our weekend to you. I'm outta here, man."

"No wait! Please don't go!" he screamed.

"Nate. Nate wake up."

Nate opened his eyes and came face to face with Ryan. *Thank god.*

"Bad dream?" Rio asked.

He nodded. "No one came. All this work and no one was at the celebration." He didn't divulge the rest, although Garron's words continued to haunt him.

"It's gonna be great, baby. Everything you touch turns out fantastic." Rio tried to comfort Nate with sprinkled kisses down his neck to his chest.

Nate buried his fingers in Rio's thick hair and directed him further south. He may be too tired to fuck, but he'd never turned down a blowjob in his life. "What if something goes wrong?"

Rio lifted his head. "I've been doing this for years. Believe me, nothing will go wrong."

Nate chuckled and tugged on a black handful of curls. "I was talking about this weekend and you know it."

"This weekend will take care of itself. Right now I'm taking care of you," Rio told him.

"You mean we're taking care of him," Ryan added, joining Rio down at Nate's groin.

Nate spread his thighs to accommodate both men. He tried to concentrate on the pleasurable tongue bath his balls and cock were receiving, but his to-do list would not let him truly enjoy it.

"Bite me," Nate suddenly ordered.

Both men stopped and gazed up at him. "Excuse me?" Ryan asked.

"Bite me. Take me outta my head. Please. Just for one night."

Ryan's teeth were the first to sink into his flesh. His lover got him on the inner thigh below his balls. The hair on Nate's body stood on end. *Fuck.* "Again."

He could detect whispering going on between the two men at his crotch but couldn't make out what they were saying. "Uh...guys?"

Rio grunted his displeasure, but Ryan bit Nate again. Instead of joining in, Rio chose to swallow Nate's cock to the root.

The dual sensation of pain and pleasure did the trick. Nate planted his heels into the mattress and thrust up, fucking Rio's mouth as Ryan continued assaulting him with his teeth. Nate knew he'd be bruised as hell by morning, but he wasn't planning to flash anyone other than the men in his bed, so he didn't worry about it.

Rio hooked his arm under one of Nate's knees and lifted, raising Nate's foot from the bed. He almost protested until he felt the scrape of Ryan's teeth across his hole.

"Fuck!" Nate howled as he shot down Rio's throat.

Panting, he gazed down at his lovers. After milking Nate's balls dry, Rio started kissing Ryan, the two of them passing his seed back and forth between them.

"Damn, that's hot," Nate said around an escaped yawn.

Still kissing, Rio and Ryan moved together up the length of Nate's body. Without a word spoken, the two men's mouths came down on Nate's. He didn't care what anyone said, tasting your own seed was sexy as fuck.

The swapping eventually died down, and Rio began petting Nate's chest. "Sleep, baby."

Nate yawned. "What about the two of you?"

Ryan shook his head. "This was about you."

Nate reached down and held the two throbbing erections in his hands. "Are you going to try and tell me you're gonna let these go to waste?"

"We can save them for breakfast. The important thing is that you know we love you. Now go to sleep and think about that instead of the celebration." Rio wrapped an arm around Nate and settled him against his chest.

Nate snuggled in and sighed. "I love you two."

He knew he still needed to come clean with his men, but there would be time later for that.

Chapter Five

"Give me a taste," Nate begged.

Rio raised a brow and looked down at his little man. "What'll you give me?"

"Anything you want," Nate answered.

"Anything?"

Nate licked his lips. "Anything. Anytime."

"You'll spoil your dinner."

"That's okay. After the breakfast you fed me earlier, I didn't have lunch," Nate chuckled.

It had been a long time since Rio had seen Nate so carefree. He wasn't sure if his man finally realised Cattle Valley Days was out of his hands or what, but Rio loved it. Reluctantly, he leaned closer. "Just lick it. No biting."

Nate rolled his eyes and grabbed Rio's wrist, bringing the ice cream cone to his mouth. He swirled that cute pink tongue of his through the sweet cream and moaned. "I need one of those."

"So get yourself one."

"Can't. I have to go pull raffle tickets. You bought some, right?"

"Yep, just like you told me to. Though what we're gonna do with a moped is anyone's guess."

"It's not the moped that's important. It's the money raised for the home that took care of Gracie until she came here." Nate bumped hips with Rio. "But I would like to win the trip to Hawaii."

"You and me, both."

Nate finally released his hold on Rio's cone and stood on his toes to plant a sweet kiss on Rio's lips. "What time is your next game?"

"Five."

"Okay. I'll be there. Sorry I missed the first one, but I got caught up with the whole bus route confusion."

"That's okay. You do what you need to do, and we'll be around when you're done." Well, at least he'd be around. Ryan had taken off again. Rio wasn't sure if it was business, or a few drinks with their friends.

He gave Nate one last kiss before his lover jogged away. Rio took his cone and found a seat under one of the shade trees.

He spotted Mario and waved him over. "You win?"

Mario shook his head and took a seat next to Rio. "Lost seven to five. What about you?"

"We won."

"Congratulations, old man," Mario teased as he punched Rio in the arm.

Something in the distance seemed to catch Mario's attention, and he immediately stopped laughing. Rio glanced over and realised it wasn't a *something*, but a *someone*.

"Asa's back in town, I see."

Mario nodded, not bothering to take his eyes off the rumoured playboy millionaire. Asa was looking pretty damn good in a pair of blue jeans and a bright red golf shirt, the man's dark hair perfectly in place despite the hot summer day.

"Go talk to him."

Mario shook his head. "He's holding court, can't you tell? Look at 'em, fawning all over him."

The crowd around Asa did indeed appear to be doing their fair share of fawning. Rio watched as Asa spotted Mario. The two men stared at each other for several moments before Asa returned his attention to his adoring group of young men.

Rio wanted to tell Mario to go over and stake his claim, but who was he to give relationship advice? Hell, he didn't know from one day to the next how his own home life was going.

Mario stood. "I'm gonna check out the rest of the carnival. Wanna come?"

Did he? No, not really, but he wanted to be a friend to Mario. "Sure."

* * * *

"So what's up with you lately?" Sonny asked.

Ryan continued to survey the growing crowd. He'd run back to his office after his baseball game and changed into jeans and a uniform shirt. Another two hours on street patrol and he'd be back at his office changing again for the game that evening.

"What do you mean?"

"You seem kind of distant, that's all."

"Just trying to make sure the day goes smoothly."

"That's not what I mean, and you know it. I'm talking about you, Rio and Nate. Is something going on there?"

Ryan turned to regard his friend. "Getting kinda nosey, aren't ya?"

Sonny shrugged. "Wouldn't ask if I didn't care."

Ryan knew the man was telling the truth. Since his shooting, Sonny had become one of the most genuine people he'd ever known. "I don't know. Just tired of coming in second, tired of seeing Rio mope around because he misses Nate, tired of arguing."

He felt his jaws clench. He was about to admit something to Sonny that he hadn't told anyone. "Tired of not being in charge, I guess."

"In charge?" Sonny questioned.

Ryan shrugged. Hell, it sounded stupid even to his own ears but it was how he felt. "Before Nate won this election, I was kinda the big dog in our relationship. Now that position has been passed to Nate, and I'm not sure how to deal with it."

"Why does there have to be a big dog? I'm confused."

"I'm not saying I get off on telling them what to do, but there was a time when they both seemed to really look up to me. I never had that growing up. I'll admit I kinda liked it."

Sonny reached out and held Ryan's hand. "You believe Nate and Rio think less of you now?"

"No. I'm not saying that. Maybe I'm the one who feels...less."

"Then that's something you need to work out on your own. But if you think it has something to do with

Rio and Nate, and the way they see you, you owe it to them to talk to 'em."

"Hard to say how Nate feels these days. He's been so damn busy. I mean, I get that, I really do, but it makes it hard. And Rio gets himself so worked up over the slightest argument lately that I can't talk to him about it."

Sonny elbowed Ryan in the side. "There's Rio. Why don't you try talking to him? Maybe he's feeling the same way." Sonny looked into Ryan's eyes. "What the three of you have is more important than pride or misunderstandings. You'd be a jackass to fuck it up because you don't want someone to possibly get upset."

Ryan sighed. *Damn.* He knew he should've run when he spotted Sonny coming towards him. The man made too damn much sense. He seemed to have the uncanny ability to take something complex and break it down into the lowest common denominator.

He gave Sonny's hand a squeeze before walking towards his partner. "Can I have a second?"

Rio stopped and regarded Mario. "Can I catch up with you later?"

Mario glanced at Ryan and nodded. "I'll be around."

Rio gestured to a spot of empty grass. "Wanna cop a squat?"

What Ryan wanted to talk about, he thought would be better dealt with in private. "How about going back to my office?"

Rio's big body stiffened. "Okay."

Ryan unclipped the radio from his belt. "Roy?"

"Yeah," his deputy said over the radio.

"I'm taking a break. Everything seems to be going fine."

"Okay, I'll keep my eyes open."

"Thanks." Ryan slipped the radio back onto his belt and reached for Rio's hand. "Did you eat?"

Rio nodded. "Shared an ice cream cone with Nate earlier."

At least his lover had something in his stomach if he decided to throw up. Which reminded Ryan. "Did you ever go see the doc?"

Rio shook his head. He didn't say anything else until they made their way to Ryan's office. "It's just nerves."

Ryan led Rio over to the sofa and pulled him down beside him. "I've seen you nervous before, and you never did this. What's different?"

Rio reached up and wiped the sweat from his forehead. "I can't handle the two of you fighting. It scares me."

Ryan didn't know if he'd ever heard Rio admit to being scared about anything. "What scares you?"

"The thought of the two of you breaking up. Would I have to choose?" Rio asked.

The anguish in Rio's voice, combined with the tears filling his eyes, broke Ryan's heart. He reached out and wrapped his arms around the man he loved. "We've just hit a rough patch. That's all. I love Nate to the bottom of my soul. Why would you ever think we'd make you choose between the two of us?"

"The judge made me choose," Rio whispered as he wiped his eyes.

"What judge? When?"

"When my folks split up. My dad had the money, and he caught my mom in an affair. They went to court because they claimed to both want me. When the judge called me into his chambers and asked who I'd rather live with, I told him my dad. It wasn't that I didn't love my mom, but I knew if I chose her, dad would make our lives hell."

Ryan knew Rio's mother had died when he was young. He wondered...

"She killed herself a month later." Rio gazed into Ryan's eyes. "See why I can't choose?"

How long had he been with Rio? How could he not have known? Suddenly his feelings felt petty in comparison. He pulled Rio in for a kiss, pushing his tongue deep into his lover's mouth. "I love you. The family that I have with you and Nate means more to me than anything."

"Really?"

Ryan nodded. "I've been acting like a jerk lately because I got caught up in self pity. If I'd known about..." Ryan kissed his way from Rio's lips to his ear. "I didn't realise how much Nate's winning that damn election would affect me."

Rio pulled back. "He hasn't said anything, but I think Nate feels the same way. I think that's what all these dreams are about, and why he's working himself to death."

"You think?" Ryan asked.

"Yeah, I do. It didn't really dawn on me until his last nightmare, but yeah, I think I'm right. I've even been considering selling *The Gym* to Mario."

"*The Gym*? Why? You love that place." Goddamn they were a fucked up bunch.

"I did love it. Now every time I walk in and don't see Nate's goofy smile, I get depressed. It's not the same, and I hate it."

"Who would've thought one job change could cause all these hurt feelings?" Ryan put his feet up on the couch and adjusted Rio to lie beside him. "Can I just hold you for awhile? I should get back out there, but I need this more than anything right now."

"You can hold me forever."

"I plan to."

* * * *

Nate raced across the grass towards the baseball fields. He'd gotten held up at the rodeo preliminaries and had lost track of time. *Shit.* He hoped he'd at least get to see the last half of the game.

The Goods and their families were taking full advantage of one of the many surrounding shade trees. Nate came to a stop and braced his hands on his knees. "What've I missed?" he panted.

Ryker glanced up from the blanket on which he, Ranger and Lilly were lying. "They're down by three, top of the seventh."

"Crap. They're gonna kill me. I promised I'd be here."

"And you are," Garron said and gestured to an empty lawn chair. "Sit down and enjoy yourself for a few minutes."

Nate took the offered seat. "Gladly. This is the last item on my to-do list for the day."

"Well, we've got nothing to compare it to, of course, but we've had a fantastic time so far. You should be proud of yourself."

Rawley's words shocked him. The hard-nosed man wasn't known for his compliments.

"Thanks. After clean-up on Sunday, I'm planning to sleep for a week."

"Maybe you should take a vacation," Jeb added to the conversation.

"Only if I can wrestle that trip to Hawaii away from Guy. Hell, it's not like the man needs a free trip. He's got more money than he knows what to do with."

Garron started laughing. "So do you, smartass. Release the purse strings and take your family to the islands for a couple weeks."

Nate's jaw dropped. He'd become so accustomed to looking for ways to save the city money, he'd completely forgotten he had plenty of his own. *Fuck me.* "I might just do that."

"Maybe you could look Quade up while you're there," Garron put in.

"Yeah, maybe."

The crowd started cheering and Nate stood. "What'd I miss?"

"That number thirty-two just hit a homer," Ranger told him. "Nice ass on him, by the way."

Nate grinned. "That's Hearn, and you're right. He's got a damn nice ass."

He watched Hearn cross the plate and jog to the fence to give Tyler and Gracie kisses. Nate tried to picture Hearn as mayor. Would he let the stress of the job interfere with his family? *No.*

"Mayor Gills?" a soft voice said from behind.

Nate grinned and glanced over his shoulder. "Jay, how many times have I told you to call me Nate?"

Jay blushed and looked down. "Several. I...um, wanted to introduce you to someone."

Nate noticed a thin young man behind Jay. He stood and gestured to an adjacent shaded area. He held out his hand to the guy. "I'm Nate Gills, and you are..."

"Ethan. Ethan Drake."

"Ethan's a friend of mine from back home. He took the bus from DC to surprise me."

Nate immediately went on alert. He wondered if this was the punk who'd been stalking and beating the shit out of Jay. He studied Jay for a few moments but couldn't read him. "Is this your ex?"

Jay's normally fair complexion paled even further. "No! As far as I know Randy still doesn't know where I am. Ethan used to volunteer at the shelter. He worked as a clerk for the Family Services Administration." Jay turned to Ethan. "Tell him."

Ethan appeared as timid as Jay, but the young man finally spoke. "There's this guy that came in one day yelling about how we took away his family. I was filling in at the front desk while the usual woman took her break. The guy, Jim, got it in his head that I'd tell him where they were. Since we usually deal with family violence, I knew there was no way I could help him. I tried to tell him that, but he grabbed me by the shirt. He told me if I didn't tell him, he'd make me sorry."

"Did you go to the police?"

Ethan nodded. "I filed a complaint. The police went by the guy's house, but he'd been evicted." Ethan took a deep breath. "I've only seen him a couple of times since, but I think he followed me home one evening. When I left for work the next morning, I found a dead cat in the hall outside my apartment. I knew the police couldn't do anything about someone they couldn't find, so I panicked. I scraped together what little money I had and hopped a bus out here."

"I told him how nice everyone was. I hope that's okay?" Once again, Jay looked worried.

"It's fine. Did you call the police in DC and tell them about the cat?"

Ethan nodded. "I called them before getting on the bus. I told them I was moving here."

Nate nodded. "You got a place to stay?"

"Jay said I could sleep on his sofa until I found a place."

With his hand shielding the glare, Nate surveyed the crowd. "Come with me."

Sitting on the bottom bleacher of the small grandstand was Kyle. "Hey, can I talk to you about something?" Nate asked, sitting beside his friend.

"Sure. What's up?"

"Did your assistant ever find a house?"

"Yeah. He moved out a couple of months ago, why?" Kyle asked.

Nate gestured to Ethan, who was standing back with Jay. "A friend of Jay's just came into town. He needs a cheap place to live. I don't know the kid personally, but Jay seems to think a lot of him. I guess he did volunteer work at the shelter where Jay used to live."

"Good enough for me. Although I'd like to have a few days to seal the elevator shaft. It's not that I don't trust the guy, but I'd rather someone who wasn't working for me didn't have access to the bakery."

"I can understand that. So what do you think? A week?"

Kyle nodded. "A week sounds good. Tell him to come by the bakery on Monday around ten. I'll give him the keys and let him take a look around."

Nate gave Kyle's shoulder a squeeze. "Thanks."

Kyle shrugged. "Don't thank me. That's what this town's about."

The words were like a punch to the stomach. Leave it to Kyle to remind him of the reason he and his partners had moved to Cattle Valley in the first place. "Yeah. You're exactly right about that."

After filling Jay and Ethan in on his conversation with Kyle, he sent them off and went back to his friends.

Garron was shaking his head when Nate arrived. "You've missed it. They're one out away from losing the game."

"Shit."

"At least they know you're here. I spotted Rio eyeing you earlier."

"A good eyeing or a bad eyeing?" Nate asked.

Garron chuckled. "Depends on what you call good. I seem to recall seeing him brush at the front of his pants a couple of times."

Nate grinned. "Oh, good."

He watched as Ryan came up to bat. At least he'd get to see one of his men in action. The crack of the bat sounded perfect. Nate stood and watched the small white ball as it flew through the air in a high arc.

"Damn," Ranger cursed before the ball even came down.

Ranger must know a hell of a lot more than Nate did because a moment later, Matt Jeffries caught the ball. A mixture of groans and whoops of joy wound their way through the crowd of fans.

Nate turned and folded the lawn chair before leaning it against the tree.

He took several steps and waited. After shaking the hands of the opposing team, a very dirty and sweaty pair of men came towards him, and they had never looked more gorgeous. He knew it was customary to go to O'Brien's after the game, but Nate wondered if he could talk his men into taking him home. Perhaps a night of hot sex was in their future.

"Sorry you lost," he said, giving Rio and Ryan consolatory kisses.

"That's okay. Just means we can take it easy on Sunday," Ryan said.

Nate bit his lip. It wasn't the time to bring up the fact that he'd have to help with clean-up on Sunday. He'd wait until after his planned night of debauchery.

"You guys heading to O'Brien's?" Rawley asked.

"Yep. A nice cold beer sounds perfect," Ryan answered.

Everyone loaded up their borrowed blankets and chairs and put them in the back of Rio's pickup. As soon as they were squeezed into the front seat, Nate put a hand over both men's cocks.

"Would you mind if we had a couple beers and made it an early night? I'm feeling exceptionally frisky for some reason." He finished the statement by groping the growing bulges under his hands.

"Damn, baby. Maybe we should run by *The Gym* and get in a little mat time before we head to the pub," Rio moaned.

Nate gave Rio's cock an extra squeeze. "Go the long way through town."

Before Rio even made it out of the parking lot, Nate had the zipper down on his uniform pants and his jock pushed to the side. He pressed his lips to his lover's crown and spread the tasty pre-cum over them.

As he slowly swallowed Rio's length, Nate felt Ryan's fingers pressing against the seam of his jeans. The truck swerved a bit, and he heard Ryan tell Rio to head to the parking lot behind *The Gym*.

Nate smiled around the fat cock stretching his lips. It had been a long time since they'd had a dirty truck fuck, as Ryan called them.

A hard right by Rio and Nate bumped his head on the steering wheel. He came up for air. "More of that and we'll get pulled over by the cops. Wouldn't that be perfect, a business owner, the sheriff and the town mayor locked up for lewd behaviour?"

Rio put a hand to the back of Nate's head and guided him down once more. "You just let me do the driving. You've got more important things to do."

A slight bump as Rio turned into the parking lot, and within seconds, the truck was in park and the seat pushed back. Although it had been a while, Nate knew just what to do. He reached down and helped Ryan remove his jeans before tucking his knees up under his chest.

The sound of the glove box being opened signalled Ryan's quest for lube. He swirled his tongue around

Rio's head and came back up for air. "Need it, Sheriff."

"I know. I think we all do," Ryan said as he spread a liberal amount of slick on Nate's hole. "Not gonna stretch you. I want you to feel my cock all day tomorrow."

Ryan knelt behind Nate, squeezing in between the door and Nate's ass. It was the wide bulbous head that first touched his hole. *Holy Shit.* Ryan really wasn't going to stretch him.

Nate wrapped his hand around the base of Rio's cock. If he was pushed forward by Ryan's meat, he didn't want to gag himself on Rio's. He felt like he'd licked an electrical socket when Ryan pressed his way inside. Nate couldn't decide if he liked the feeling or not. One thing was for sure. He'd definitely feel it for days.

Once Ryan was fully seated, Nate began administering to Rio's cock once again. He got his fingers involved after reaching behind himself to catch some of the excess lube. *Damn.* Ryan must've thought he looked rusty with all he'd squirted back there.

As he sucked Rio's fat head, he worked his lover's hole. With every thrust of Ryan's hips, Nate took Rio deeper into his mouth. Without the ability to tell Ryan how good the fucking was, Nate settled for a series of loud moans and whimpers, which Rio seemed to greatly appreciate.

At one point, the sounds of slapping skin and moans of ecstasy were so loud in the closed confines of the truck, Nate almost covered his ears. Yep. This was exactly the kind of dirty truck fuck he'd been looking forward to.

Rio was the first to slip over the edge, although Nate had a feeling it was the third finger he'd introduced that had done the pushing. With Rio collapsed against the driver's door, Nate reached down and wrapped his hand around his own erection. He gave Ryan his full attention as his lover's hips pistoned back and forth.

When Rio's thumb pressed against the slit on Nate's crown, he completely lost it, spraying the seat and their hands with the thick, white cream.

"Shit. Shit. Oh fuck, I'm coming," Ryan howled.

Nate felt Ryan's body jerk against him as he emptied his seed.

It wasn't until he'd regained his breath that Nate noticed the overwhelming smell of sex in the cab. Although the air conditioning was running full blast, Nate reached across Rio's lap and rolled down the window.

He collapsed against Rio's thighs and wished for nothing but a good night's sleep. It was Rio's cell phone going off that woke him several moments later.

"Hello?"

"Oh, yeah. We'll be there. No. No. We just got a little sidetracked. Okay, see ya then."

Rio ran the back of his hand over Nate's jaw. "They wanted to know where we were."

Nate opened his eyes and sat up. He was sure they all smelled like sex. "Let's run inside and clean up first."

"Sounds like a plan," Rio agreed.

Ryan gave a grunt and pulled his baseball pants back on.

"Two drinks, right? Then we can leave?" Nate asked, making sure they were all on the same page.

"Yep. If we even make it to two." Ryan winked and opened the passenger door.

Nate began to hatch a plan to get his lovers horny enough to leave early. Shouldn't be too hard, he was a professional when it came to flirting.

* * * *

"So, no bull riding this year, huh?" Rio asked Jeremy Lovell. Before he could answer, Nate once again ran a hand up the inside of his thigh. Rio squeezed his legs together, trapping the tormenting hand.

Jeremy laughed and shook his head. "Nope. I've found something even better than the adrenaline rush I got from a good bull ride."

Rio watched Jeremy glance at Shep. *Yeah.* He knew that feeling. There was a time when he couldn't imagine anything more exciting than wandering the jungle, protecting his clients. Now, he had all the excitement a man could ever need. "I get that."

He finished off his beer and poured another from the pitcher between him and Nate. He bumped shoulders with his lover. "Better drink up."

A sleepy-looking Nate began chugging the warm beer in his glass before pouring himself another. "You do know I have to be up and out of the house by five, right?"

Rio glanced at the large Coca-Cola sign on the wall. Even if they left in the next few minutes, it would only give his partner about five hours of sleep. On the other side of Nate, Ryan was involved in a lively discussion about tattoos with Kade.

He leaned over and whispered in Nate's ear. "Why don't you give Ryan some of the attention you've been paying me? That'll light a fire under his ass."

"Or in his crotch," Nate said with a chuckle.

Rio turned back to Shep. "Heard you had a problem on the ranch last week?"

Shep shook his head. "Yeah. I still can't believe I did that."

"You should've seen him. He was like a man possessed," Jeremy laughed.

"Should've just sold the mean sonofabitch." Shep gazed at Jeremy. "What can I say, I'm a man ruled by passion, and at that moment my passion was to see Zero dead and buried."

Someone thumped Rio on the back of the head. He spun around ready for a fight, and came face to face with Ryan's hard cock trapped behind the zipper of his uniform pants. He followed the sexy length of his lover's body until they made eye contact. Yep. He could see the lust written all over Ryan.

"Nate needs to get home."

Rio grinned. "Okay." He turned back to Jeremy and Shep. "We'll probably catch up with you all at the rodeo."

After waving goodbye to the rest of his friends, Rio strode towards the door. He couldn't keep a chuckle from erupting when he spotted Ryan practically pushing Nate out of the bar. Nate must've done a damn good job of convincing Ryan it was bedtime.

Chapter Six

With Ryan beside him, and Rio behind the wheel of the vintage convertible, Nate waved to the people lining Main Street. "Where'd all these people come from?"

"Hell if I know. Guess word's gotten around over the years. This is by far the biggest crowd I've ever seen in Cattle Valley," Ryan answered.

Despite the friendly smile plastered on his face, Nate began to mentally calculate the supplies he'd ordered. "If all these people come to the dance, I won't have enough seating. That's not such a big deal, but I gave Sean and Erico an estimate of the number of people, so they're not gonna have enough food and drink."

He heard Ryan reassure him that everything would be fine, but Nate was too busy beating himself up over the failure.

As soon as they got to the end of the parade route, Nate slumped down in the seat and covered his face as he finally allowed himself to break down in tears.

"Hey, hey," Ryan said, pulling Nate into his lap. "Don't let this upset you."

"You don't understand. I should've known I couldn't do this. I'm a total fuck-up as a mayor, but I thought I could at least put on a good celebration. That's all I wanted. I was hoping if people enjoyed themselves more than they ever had, they'd cut me some slack when it came to my other duties."

Rio continued to drive until they were between the town and the rodeo grounds before he pulled onto a side road. He stopped the car and crawled into the backseat with Nate and Ryan.

Nate's big strong lovers gave him the sweetest kisses as they worked to calm him down.

"Is this what's been botherin' ya all this time?" Rio asked.

Nate nodded. "I didn't want you guys to know what a fuck-up I was. I couldn't let people help me, because I was afraid they'd see how unqualified I am for this job." He threw up his hands in despair. "And now all my work will be for nothing, because I'll have a mob of hungry people without anywhere to sit on my hands, and it'll all be my fault."

"Oh, baby," Rio tried to soothe him. "We'll help."

"I'll get one of the big city trucks and drive into Sheridan. Surely there are more tables and chairs we can rent. I'll get the Good brothers, Garron and Jeb to help. We'll take care of it. I promise."

Lifting his gaze to make eye contact with the men he loved had him crying even harder. "I'm so sorry I didn't tell you. I don't know why you put up with me."

"Because you're our Nate, and we love you," Rio whispered against Nate's tear stained cheek.

"Now dry those eyes. You've got a rodeo to preside over, and I've got some tables to find."

"Can you stop by, or call Sean, and ask him about the food and beer?"

"I'll take care of it." Ryan held Nate under his chin and kissed him. "When we stick together, we make a pretty damn good team."

"So why can't we seem to remember that?" Rio chimed in.

Nate lifted the bottom of his golf shirt and used the underside to dry his face. His breathing was still erratic from the episode, but at least the crying jag was coming to an end. He knew the three of them would need to sit down after all this was over and have a serious talk about his future in politics.

Ryan and Rio continued to pet and soothe Nate until he was completely calmed down. "I need to get to the rodeo," he mumbled.

He wasn't looking forward to being in the announcer's box, but it was expected. Nate hoped he wasn't supposed to talk and joke around with the announcer, because he really didn't know if he'd be able to pull that off.

At least Rio would be down below taking tickets and acting as one of his gate keepers. He knew if he needed him, Rio would drop everything for him. "Okay. Let's do this thing."

Rio gave him another kiss. When he started to pull away, Nate held on and kissed him again, thrusting his tongue into his lover's mouth.

Rio groaned and started to take things further, but a clearing throat stopped them. Nate pulled his tongue out of Rio's mouth and grinned. "A little something to get me through the day."

Ryan started to chuckle, and, before long, they were all laughing. Nate felt better by the time Rio climbed back into the front seat and put the car into gear. He may not be fit to be mayor, but his men loved him regardless.

* * * *

"So, I assume since we're making this run, Nate finally talked to you?" Garron asked.

Driving the truckload of eight foot long banquet tables, Ryan glanced in the rear view mirror to make sure Ranger was keeping up with him. They'd left Sonny, Jeb and Lilly to get the extra tables and chairs from the church recreation hall while they made the trip.

"Yeah," Ryan finally replied. He shook his head. "I had no idea things were so bad for him."

"Whatever you do, don't let him quit."

Ryan took his eyes off the road long enough to give Garron a narrowed gaze. "I'll support him no matter what he decides. I've never seen him like he was earlier. No job is worth that."

"Maybe not, but I think Nate's just suffering from lack of self-confidence. He has the intelligence and the people skills to do that job, and we both know it."

"Could you watch Sonny do something that made him miserable?"

"Yep. I did. When he was working his way through physical therapy, it killed me to watch him struggle and suffer, but I continued to push because I knew it was the right thing to do. Don't think I didn't have days when I just wanted to sit and hold him, and protect him from the world. Look, all you can do is give him all the love and support you can, while still pushing him to do the right thing."

Ryan knew Sonny had had a rough time after he'd been shot in the head. Nate had talked to Garron almost daily during Sonny's rehabilitation. Maybe he should listen to what Garron was trying to tell him. It felt to Ryan like he was riding a fence. He wanted to give Nate what he needed to be happy again, but at the same time, he knew Nate would never be the same if he just gave up.

"I'll think about it," he agreed.

He'd been lucky enough to get the beer distributor on the phone before they'd made the run out to Cattle Valley. He'd been even luckier when the guy told him he had enough to bring him an additional ten kegs of beer. Ryan figured if that wasn't enough, it would be too damn bad. As it was, it didn't sit well with him. Was it even ethical for a sheriff to supply an entire town with free-flowing alcohol? Once again the answer came back to Nate. It may not be the smartest thing he'd ever done, but he'd do it again if it helped his lover.

As they drove by the rodeo grounds, Ryan could hear the screaming crowd even with the windows up. "Must be a helluva show."

He was disappointed he wasn't going to be able to catch it this year. He'd been to every rodeo since he'd moved to town.

Garron whistled. "What I wanna know is, how they packed all those people in there? They got cars parked clear out here by the road."

Ryan tried to turn a blind eye to all the illegally parked vehicles. *It's one day a year.* "Hopefully we'll have time to get this stuff set up before the thing's over. I called Roy and asked him to get another two blocks cleared of cars and closed down. I don't know what we're going to do if we still don't have enough room."

"We'll figure it out." Garron laid a supportive hand on Ryan's shoulder.

"We're gonna have to."

* * * *

Still at the gate he'd been assigned, Rio had found a wire crate and turned it upside down to use for a stool. The rodeo was almost over, and, so far, the darn thing had managed to hold him. One of the out-of-town cowboys was set to ride Satan's Bandit, and so far no one had been able to stay on the mean sonofabitch for the full eight seconds.

The cowboy was still in the chute trying to get his hold just right. The tension in the air was so thick, the crowd had gone completely quiet. Rio wiped the sweat from his forehead as he watched the gate fly open and Satan's Bandit come flying out, kicking like his name sake were on his tail.

Although it was close a time or two, the cowboy managed to stay seated until the eight second buzzer sounded. The crowd behind him erupted in applause. When the judges' scores came up as the highest of the day, the people went nuts, stamping their feet, hollering and jumping up and down. An unnatural sound caught Rio's attention, he surveyed the screaming crowd, trying to figure out what it was. He made eye contact with Nate up in the box and waved. He chuckled as the announcer seemed to get into the spirit of the moment. The gaudy sequined cowboy shirt almost blinded Rio every time the red haired man jumped in the air.

Before Nate could lift his arm to return the gesture, a loud popping sound echoed throughout the arena. Rio's eyes widened as he watched the box his lover was in begin to fall, along with an entire large section of the grandstand. Screams from those suddenly falling mixed with the celebrating crowd.

The entire collapse lasted mere seconds. Rio was momentarily stunned as he searched the pile of debris for the white box Nate had been ensconced in. As he pushed off the crate and started running to the catastrophe, he pulled the cell phone out of his pocket and called Ryan.

"Hey," Ryan answered.

"The grandstand collapsed. Get every emergency vehicle you can out here, now!"

"Wait! Are people hurt?" Ryan asked, his voice frantic.

"Some worse than that I'm afraid, by the looks of things. I gotta go find Nate." Rio hung up without waiting for a reply and shoved the phone back into his pocket.

"Nate!" he called as he headed for the remains of the announcer's booth.

The structure had partially broken apart on impact. Rio carefully made his way to the top of the heap and began sifting through the broken boards. He caught sight of a sequined shirt. Moving quickly, he uncovered Earl Graves, the announcer. *Fuck.* It was obvious by the man's twisted neck that he was dead. Fear filled Rio. Although others were screaming for help, Rio's focus was on getting Nate.

"Nate!" he called again as he moved another section of the booth.

"Here!" Nate yelled back.

Rio saw a hand stick up from around a door. He picked the slab of wood up like it weighed nothing and carefully tried to move it to the side. All around him cries of pain and anguish could be heard.

His first glimpse of Nate's bloody face nearly stopped his heart. Rio tried to shut out the chaos while trying to figure how to get his love out of the debris without hurting him further.

"Just get this board off my leg and help me up," Nate said, calmer than Rio had expected.

He lifted the board and set it aside, knowing it was possible someone was buried beneath where he was stacking the broken wood. He shook the images off Earl and focused once again on Nate, who reached out and grabbed Rio's arm. "I'm okay. Just lift me up."

Rio didn't know whether or not to follow Nate's instructions. What if Nate was hurt worse than he knew? What if by lifting him out, Rio inadvertently hurt him more?

"Rio! Snap out of it and help me up!" Nate screamed at him.

With a deep breath, Rio carefully lifted Nate into his arms. He stared at his man's bloody face, arms and legs. "You're hurt."

Nate shook his head. "Nothing I won't live through, but there are others who need our help."

A particularly bad cut on Nate's arm caught Rio's attention. Without thinking, he tore the T-shirt from his body and ripped it into several strips, which he used as a makeshift bandage.

"We need to get these people out of here. Did you find anyone else from the booth?"

Rio blinked several times, the activity around him finally catching his full attention. How would Nate react if he told him the truth? "I found Earl." He shook his head. "He's dead."

"What? Did you get him out?" Nate asked.

"No. Everything's so unstable. I'm afraid the more I dig, the more I'm likely to hurt someone. I don't know where to begin."

Nate held one hand over his bleeding arm as he surveyed the area. Rio watched as his lover wiped a few stray tears from his cheeks. "Let's start over there at the edge. We can work our way in and down from there."

On their way over to the edge of the collapsed bleachers, Rio stopped to help Pam Gleeson to her feet. "Where're the boys?" he asked, thinking of her two young sons being buried in the rubble.

Pam shook her head and pointed towards the concession stand. "They wanted popcorn," she cried and covered her mouth. "I let them go by themselves. I...I thought they'd be save enough."

Pam started to sink to her knees, but Rio kept her on her feet and passed her off to a waiting man he didn't even know. Pam clung to the man for dear life. "What if they were on their way back up?" Pam continued to cry.

Rio turned away and took a deep breath. He knew before the day was out, his emotions would be tested to their limits. If he didn't get control over himself, he wouldn't be good for anybody.

He spotted Nate speaking calmly to a woman, who appeared trapped between the fallen section of grandstand and the still-standing one. How could his lover appear so calm?

Come on, Ryan. We need you.

* * * *

As Ryan sped towards the rodeo grounds, he called the Wyoming State Police office in Sheridan and explained what had happened. "I'm pulling up to the scene now. Our ambulance was already on hand in case one of the riders was injured."

"We'll coordinate things on this end," the dispatcher told him.

"Holy fuck," he whispered as he got his first glimpse at the carnage. "Send as many helicopters as you can. It's worse than I thought."

"I'll put in the calls."

Ryan hung up and handed his phone to Garron. "If they call back, you'll have to talk to them. Tell 'em you're a sheriff in Nebraska and they won't give you any shit."

Garron nodded and stuck the phone in his front pocket. "What do you want us to do?"

Ryan couldn't believe all the activity going on in front of him. "Anything you can."

It was easy to spot Rio from his position towards the top of the pile of rubble. Had he found Nate? A hole seemed to open inside him at the thought of Rio searching for Nate by himself.

As he made his way through the debris, he assured people that help was on the way. Several times injured friends and neighbours reached out to him for assistance. Ryan did what he could, but moved away quickly once they were safe.

"Rio!" he yelled.

Rio stopped what he was doing and looked up, meeting Ryan's gaze. He pointed to the left.

Ryan followed the gesture, his eyes roaming the sea of injured people until they landed on Nate. "Thank God."

He continued to watch Nate for several moments to make sure he was okay. Nate appeared to be handling the accident better than anyone. He was sure as hell a lot calmer than everyone else. Ryan briefly wondered if his lover could be in shock.

A comforting smile transformed Nate's bloody face to one of hope. Nate was fine. Ryan took a deep cleansing breath. It appeared as though there were plenty of people already actively searching for the injured, so Ryan decided to put his field training to use.

He made his way down to the ambulance. Zac Alban was inserting an IV into Ezra James. Wyn stood next to his partner, his face paler than the moon in the night sky. Ryan glanced at Zac. The paramedic must've understood the unspoken question.

"He's had a minor heart attack, but I think he should be okay if we can get him to the hospital. I've got his vitals under control. Do you know how far out help is?"

Ryan shook his head. "I told 'em to send helicopters."

Zac shook his head. "From what I've seen, we're gonna need a hell of a lot of 'em, plus a fleet of ambulances to transfer these people."

"Where are the docs?" Ryan asked.

"Nate already called them. They're setting up the clinic for the walking wounded."

Ryan scratched at his jaw. "We can start loading people on one of the busses in the parking lot. We'll have to set up an area where we can try and assess people's injuries. The cuts and scrapes can go into the clinic. That'll free up the helicopters and ambulances for the more seriously injured."

Zac nodded his agreement. "Nate's already started setting up an area over by the parking lot. You might see if you can find George or Collin Zeffer. They've both been trained in triage."

"Got it." Ryan spun around and searched the crowd. He wished he had his sheriff's vehicle with him. At least then he'd have a bullhorn. He was proud of Nate for keeping his cool in the situation.

He strode over to the crowd and cupped his hands around his mouth. "Collin Zeffer! George Manning!" he shouted as he walked through the throng of injured people.

"Here!" Collin yelled, waving his arms as he tried to make his way to Ryan.

"Where's George?" Ryan asked.

"I don't know. I tried to call him earlier, but he's not answering his phone."

Ryan looked at the pile of debris. "Was he here?"

Collin shook his head. "I don't think so. Trick was supposed to come into town earlier. He's probably with him."

Shit. Ryan knew the two men were old school friends. They could be anywhere. "Okay. I need you to go help Zac. Nate's set up a triage area. The people that have minor injuries will be bussed to the clinic. I'll see if I can find the driver and have him move the bus as close as possible."

He heard a helicopter overhead. "Okay. Let's get moving. I'll keep trying to get George on the phone."

Collin nodded. It wasn't until he started to move off that he spotted Abe. He could tell the reclusive man was uncomfortable in the chaotic atmosphere. "Why don't you go with Collin," Ryan said to Abe.

"Thanks."

It didn't take Ryan long to find the hired bus driver. He was working right alongside everyone else to get as many people uncovered as possible. Ryan explained what the plan was and sent the man on his way.

Since discovering Nate was safe, Ryan had slipped into rescue mode. It wasn't until he saw the vacant stare of Gavin Lively that it all became real to him.

Ryan knelt and bowed his head. He didn't need to touch the young man to know he was dead. Tears sprung to Ryan's eyes. These were his friends. The people he said hi to every day. How many would end up like the young man who ran Wyn's store?

Ryan was caught between what he wanted to do and what he should do. Finally going with his gut instinct, he lifted the steel bars that covered Gavin's body. Once cleared of the twisted metal, Ryan came face to face with the fatal head wound that had ended the once happy man's life. He quickly looked around to make sure he wasn't drawing a crowd and closed the dead man's eyes. "Sleep," he whispered.

He took a deep breath and pulled off his shirt. He wrapped the khaki sheriff's department garment around Gavin's head and lifted the body from the rubble. Once clear of the crowd, he surveyed the area.

"Ryan?"

"Don't come over here, Nate." He purposely stood with his back to his lover.

"Is he dead?" Although Nate's voice was controlled, Ryan could hear the anguish of the day hidden below.

"Yes. I need to find somewhere to lay him down."

Without a word, Nate strode past him towards the horse trailers. He glanced back and gestured for Ryan to follow.

"I can take care of this. Why don't you go back and help the others."

Nate shook his head. They continued to journey around the trailers until they came to a small shade tree. "Here. Put him next to Earl," Nate said, gesturing to an area beside another partially covered body.

Ryan laid Gavin's body in the cooler temperature of the shade and straightened the man's body.

Nate knelt beside Ryan. "Who is it?"

Ryan realised it was the first time Nate had asked the question. It said a lot about his lover. To Nate it could've been anyone who deserved the respect of privacy and shade in death. Ryan knew Gavin's death wasn't going to come easy for his lover. Nate practically kept Wynfields's Department Store in business, and Gavin had become a partner in crime for his monthly shopping trips.

Nate's hand landed on Ryan's bare arm. "Ryan?"

"Gavin."

Nate's hand squeezed the flesh under it. "Neil's been looking for him."

"Neil Peters?"

Nate nodded. "They've been seeing each other for a couple of months now."

Nate suddenly stood and turned back towards the chaos. Ambulances could be heard flooding the area as well as a helicopter taking off. Nate looked up. "That'll probably be Ezra. I wonder if they let Wyn ride with him?"

"I doubt it," Ryan said as he stood beside Nate.

It was an oddly serene moment. The two of them stood there for several moments without a word being spoken.

"Well, I need to find someone from the *EZ Does It* who can take care of Neil after I tell him..." Nate choked on a sob as it burst from his chest. "Our town will never be the same."

Ryan pulled Nate into his arms and kissed the top of his head. "We'll heal."

* * * *

Rio helped Ryan Bronwyn make his way to the triage area they'd set up before turning back to the pile. It had been over two hours since the collapse, and they still had people unaccounted for.

At least they'd been lucky so far. Although a lot of people were trapped in the debris, most victims only had minor injuries. There'd been a few where he wondered if they'd make it, but most, like Ryan, were suffering cuts, bruises and dehydration.

In an odd moment of quiet, Rio heard a woman's voice calling for help. His spine stiffened. He knew that voice. "Carol!"

He listened again, but another helicopter was landing nearby, drowning out any possible reply from Nate's assistant. "Quiet!" he screamed.

Rio began walking around the area with his face as close to the sharp debris as he dared. He continued to call Carol's name in hopes she would answer.

"Help me."

Rio stopped and backed up. "Carol?"

He heard something that sounded like a groan and started clearing bleacher boards and support brackets from the area. "Fuck!" he screamed when he realised he'd been standing right over the top of her.

"Can I get a stretcher over here!" he yelled.

Rio continued to slowly uncover Carol's body, making sure he didn't injure her further. *Dammit, I should've been more careful.* He couldn't help but to wonder what his weight had done to her.

It was hard to tell the extent of her injuries upon first look. "What hurts?"

Carol managed to open her eyes, squinting as the sunlight hit her face. Rio moved just enough to shield her from the bright rays and reached for her hand.

"Ca...n't...bre...athe," she panted.

He saw two paramedics working their way towards him with a backboard. "Hurry. I think she has a collapsed lung."

Rio stepped back and let the paramedics take over Carol's care. He watched them work frantically for a few moments before he turned away. He couldn't shake the feeling that he was doing more harm than good as he picked his way through the debris. No doubt he'd either caused the collapsed lung or made it worse.

Frustrated, he grabbed two handfuls of his hair and pulled. The pain brought him back to the problem at hand. A professional rescue crew had just arrived from Sheridan. Maybe it would be better to let them do their work, and just wait for further instructions.

He was on his way to find Nate when he spotted Mario. Other than a scrape on his forehead, he looked fine. Rio pulled him into a hug. "I'm glad you're all right."

Mario nodded. "I was on the grandstand that didn't collapse, but Asa wasn't so lucky."

Rio pulled back. "Is he okay?"

Mario shrugged. "I don't know. They airlifted him to Sheridan. He was in the booth with Nate. I didn't see him, and no one will tell me anything."

That could've been Nate. "Do you want me to find someone to drive you to the hospital?"

Mario shook his head. "I'm sure he has his 'people' there. He doesn't need me there."

"Maybe, maybe not, but I think you'd be better off knowing for sure, don't you?"

Jeb came into view, and Rio held up a hand to Mario. "Wait right here."

He ran over to Jeb. "Do you think you can round up another bus driver?"

"Huh?"

"There are a lot of people here who need to get to their loved ones in Sheridan. I think it'd be better if they didn't drive themselves. I know Nate has one of the busses taking injured people into Cattle Valley, but there should be another one or two around. So, can you find one of the drivers for me?"

Jeb nodded. "Sure. I'll do my best."

"Thanks. And start spreading the word to the families."

Jeb nodded again. "I'm grateful for something constructive to do. I'll admit I feel a bit lost."

Rio understood perfectly. He figured that's how they all felt. "I'll tell Mario to look for the bus."

Rio ran back over to his friend and explained what his plans were. "Don't worry about getting back. If I have to drive the damn bus myself, we'll make sure all of you are taken care of."

"Did you hear Gavin Lively's dead?" Mario asked.

"What?"

Mario nodded. "I guess Ryan found him."

"I found Earl earlier. Have there been any more?"

Mario shook his head. "I haven't heard of any more, but who knows about the people they took in the helicopters."

Mario clamped his mouth shut. Rio watched as his friend struggled to get his emotions under control, no doubt wondering about Asa. Rio pulled Mario into another hug. No words were needed, only support. He tried to give Mario as much as he needed to get himself together.

When Mario stepped back, Rio could tell he'd done just that. "Sorry," Mario mumbled.

"Don't be." He gestured off towards the parking lot. "The bus is somewhere over there. Please get on it. You'll hate yourself if you don't."

Mario nodded and walked away.

Rio wished he could cover his ears and block out the sounds of the day. He wanted nothing more than to go back in time. Should he have been keeping a count of the people filing into the grandstands? He knew there were twice as many people shoved onto the bleachers than normal. Why hadn't he considered what might happen?

He heard the siren of George Manning's Suburban as it pulled into the parking lot. It wasn't until that moment he realised it was the first of the fire chief that he'd seen. Where the hell had he been?

George jumped out of the SUV and grabbed a large first aid kit. Rio didn't miss the chief's ashen complexion, or the guilt evident in the man's eyes. Rio decided to take a chance and moved towards the upset man.

There was no proof that George and Carol had something going between them, but Rio knew they were at least close friends. He stopped George's charge through the crowd by grabbing his arm.

George spun around like he was ready to punch someone. When he realised it was Rio, his expression gentled.

"I thought you'd want to know. I pulled Carol out a few minutes ago."

"And?"

"They've already airlifted her to Sheridan."

"Is she...?"

Rio shrugged. "I don't know. She wasn't breathing very well. A collapsed lung would be my guess." He didn't tell George about the blood covering her body. From the expression on the man's face, he was barely holding himself together.

"They're getting a bus ready to take people to the hospital to sit and wait for news on their loved ones if you're interested."

George shook his head. "I can't. Not until the last person is taken out of here."

"There are professional rescue crews here now."

George nodded. "I should've been here." He squeezed his eyes shut. "Dammit! I should've been here."

"Don't do that to yourself. You couldn't have foreseen what was gonna happen."

George pulled his arm out of Rio's grasp. "I've got work to do."

Rio watched as George made his way through the mess. He knew George well enough to know something was eating away at him.

"Hey," Nate said as he wrapped his arms around Rio from behind.

Rio turned around and embraced his lover, the news of Asa once again crossing his mind. "I love you."

Nate gazed up into Rio's eyes. "I love you, too."

Rio tried to wipe some of the dried blood from Nate's face. "Have you had someone look at that arm yet?"

Nate shook his head. "It needs stitches, but it can wait."

"I heard about Gavin. I'm sorry, baby."

Nate buried his head against Rio's chest. "I had to tell Neil. I never in my life thought I'd have to look into someone's eyes and tell them the man they were falling in love with was dead."

"Is he okay?"

Nate shook his head "No. He had to be sedated. He kept demanding to see Gavin's body, but I wouldn't tell him where it was."

"That bad?"

Nate nodded. "Yeah."

Rio kissed the top of Nate's head. Gone was the perfectly mussed style his lover favoured. Nate looked like a man who'd been through hell, and Rio guessed he had, as they all had.

He surveyed their surroundings. There was still so much left to do. Hopefully the last of the injured would be uncovered in the next hour. The rescue teams were having trouble getting to the middle section of bleachers. It seemed when the grandstand collapsed, the top had basically folded over onto the middle, burying the entire section under a mountain of debris.

The sun was starting to get lower in the sky. "We should probably get the lights turned on. We might need some portable generators to add light to the specific areas the rescue guys are working on."

"We've got some at the city barn. I'll find someone to go get them. I've already called Sean. He and Erico are coordinating the food. They'll bring some out here for the rescue teams. I told them to go ahead and open Main Street for people to gather. I had to get with Ryan to have the barricades moved away from the front of the clinic. Even though the emergency entrance is around back, the bus is parking in front."

Rio was proud of the way Nate was taking control. Despite what Nate thought of his ability to be mayor, he was proving he had the right stuff when it really counted. He kept his mouth shut though. It wasn't the time or place to praise Nate's leadership skills.

"What's next?"

"I don't know. Get the lights in here, the food, set up a rest area. I need to start a list of the people injured and where they were taken." Nate glanced around. "I'll need help with that. Have you seen Carol anywhere?"

Rio felt like he'd been punched in the stomach. "I'm sorry, baby, Carol was hurt. She was airlifted to Sheridan."

Nate's face went pale. Rio felt his lover's knees begin to buckle and held him up.

"How am I supposed to do this stuff without her?"

A man carrying a news camera caught Rio's eye. "Fuck."

He pulled Nate to the side out of sight. "I should've known it was only a matter of time before the journalists started showing up."

Nate tried to look around Rio. "Why aren't the state police keeping them out?"

"I don't know, but they'll want a statement from either you or Ryan."

"Well, they'll have to wait until the last person is rescued for that."

Chapter Seven

Ryan finally found Nate sitting in one of the city trucks with a cell phone to his ear. He stood between the open door and Nate as he waited for him to end his call. Rio had run home earlier to get the car charger after all three of their phones had run out of juice.

"Okay. Keep me updated." Nate hung up and scribbled something in the spiral notebook in his hand. "That was the hospital. Carol's out of surgery."

"And?" Ryan asked.

"They're optimistic, but the doctor says it's too early to tell. She suffered a lot of internal injuries along with the punctured lung."

"Did you get news on anyone else?"

Nate glanced over his list. "Ezra should make a full recovery. Asa suffered compound fractures to both legs and a broken left clavicle. Eli Sanchez lost two fingers and will have a hell of a scar running up his arm. The doctors said they'd been lucky to save what they did."

Nate flipped the page before tossing the notebook on the seat beside him. "Four dead. Gavin, one of the cowboys from the Back Breaker, Jim Becker, Earl, and…"

Nate wouldn't meet Ryan's gaze. *Shit.* "And who?"

"Rick."

"Rick as in my deputy?"

Nate nodded.

"That can't be right. Rick called in sick. He said he had the flu." Ryan had tried to call him several times since the collapse. Flu or not, he'd needed every available set of hands.

"I'm sorry."

Ryan sat on the ground, his legs no longer able to hold him up. "Did someone call his mom?"

Nate nodded again. "Yeah. I called her."

Ida Buchanon lived in an assisted living complex in Sheridan. Ryan wondered if the staff was aware of her loss. Rick had been her only child and the light of her life. Ryan couldn't begin to understand how she must be feeling. "I'll go see her first thing in the morning."

"Reverend Sharp's holding a special service at noon. Maybe you could bring her back for that."

"Yeah."

"I'm getting ready to go into town. I think I've done all I can do here. I need to get an updated list from the clinic. Erico said everyone seems to be milling around downtown not sure what to do with themselves. I spoke with the hospital about sending grief counsellors out."

"That's good. I'm sure everyone will appreciate it. I need to stay here, but I'll find Rio to go with you."

"That's okay. You go do what you need to do. I'll find Rio."

Ryan stood and helped Nate out of the truck. He pulled Nate in his arms, mindful of the cut. Ryan once again thanked God for sparing his family. "The first thing I want you to do is have one of the docs stitch up that cut. I just hope like hell you didn't wait too long."

"If I did, I did. I'll come away with a whole lot less than most people. Although you may have to get used to me looking less than perfect." Nate tried to smile, but Ryan saw right through it.

"Do you think you deserve to be scarred? Is that why you waited?"

Nate's head tilted to the side. "What kind of man would I be if I sought treatment for myself when my friends lay buried and hurt? I waited because it was the right thing to do. It had nothing whatsoever to do with wanting a scar. I'm sure God will take care of what I deserve when the time comes."

"What's that supposed to mean?" Ryan didn't like the sound of that statement one bit.

"Nothing. I'm gonna find Rio." Nate stood on his toes and gave Ryan a quick kiss. "We'll be in town when you've finished up here."

* * * *

The waiting room was almost empty by the time Rio walked Nate into the clinic. They approached Jill, the receptionist, and Nate reached for the sign-in form.

"I need one of the docs to take a look at my arm after they've seen everyone else," Nate informed her.

Jill's tired eyes went to the bloody make-shift bandage around Nate's upper arm. "I think Isaac's available. I'll call him for you."

Nate gestured to the waiting room. "No. Take these people first."

Jill tried a smile that fell flat. "They've already been seen. I think for some reason they're finding comfort sitting in here. I don't have the heart to shoo them out."

Nate studied the faces in the room. Some he knew in passing, others were complete strangers. He doubted the out of town folks would ever step foot in Cattle Valley again after everything they'd been through.

"Nate?" Isaac called from the doorway.

Nate walked towards Isaac with Rio still at his side. "You can wait here if you want."

Rio shook his head. "No way. I've done my part for everyone else. Now it's time to make sure the man I love is okay."

Nate remembered he left his notebook in the city truck. "Shit. Will you go out and get my list outta the truck?"

"Which room will he be in, Isaac?"

"Four."

Rio nodded and gave Nate a quick kiss. "I'll be right back."

Nate knew it would take Rio several moments because they'd had to park down the block, and he wanted a few minutes with Isaac alone.

Entering the small exam room, Nate took the customary seat on the table and began to unwrap his arm. "Do you have a count on how many people you had through here?"

"Just under a hundred, I'd guess. Jill will have a final count and list of injuries for you later tomorrow. She's pretty wrung out, so I think it would be better for her to get some sleep before making sense of the sign-in sheets."

"Anything serious?" Nate knew the clinic was supposed to receive only the walking wounded, but you never know what might come up upon closer examination.

Isaac hissed when he started washing away the blood on Nate's arm. "This is pretty bad, Nate."

"I'm okay."

Isaac went quiet for a few moments. "You asked me if anything was serious? Well, take a look at your arm. This is the worst injury I've treated. Why in the hell did you let this go? Do you know how easily you could've gone into shock from the loss of blood alone?"

A noise from the doorway caught Nate's attention. Rio stood, rubbing his stomach. *Oh crap.* Was his lover getting ready to throw up?

"It's my fault," Rio mumbled. "I'm the one who got him out of there. I should've insisted he get help right away."

Isaac rolled his eyes, making a disgusted sound in his throat. "Nate's a big boy. He should've known."

Nate stared at Rio while Isaac continued to clean his wound. "Ouch. Fuck!"

Isaac stepped back, still shaking his head. "I'm going to need to deaden the area before I can even get it clean. I hope you don't have a problem with needles."

"Needles? No. I've got no problem with needles. It's the pain they cause that I take issue with." Nate held out his good hand and waited for Rio to join him beside the table.

"You okay?" he asked his big strong lover.

"Are any of us?" Rio shook his head. "I'll get through it."

Nate tried to distract himself from the series of sharp pricks into the cut on his arm. "Hey, doc, while we're here, why don't you look at Rio. He's been having a lot of stomach problems lately."

Isaac didn't take his eyes off what he was doing when he addressed Rio. "What kind of trouble?"

"Throwing up when he gets upset. Popping antacids like crazy," Nate informed Isaac.

"Stop taking antacids, you'll screw up your body. Those damn things are meant for occasional acid reflux. The best thing you can do is lay off the meat for a while. Try to stick to a diet of fruits and vegetables that have natural alkaline in them. If that doesn't help, come back in, and I'll give you some prescription medication." Isaac stepped back and disposed of the needle and syringe.

He turned to Rio and lifted a single black eye brow. "And figure out what the hell is worrying you and deal with it."

Nate watched as Rio's dark complexion went a shade of red.

"I'm trying," Rio said.

"Try harder." Isaac began cleaning Nate's wound again. "Can you feel this?"

Nate shook his head. "Will you be able to stitch it?"

"Yeah. But the way the skin appears ripped, it might not be pretty. If you'd like, I can give you the number for a good plastic surgeon in Sheridan."

"No need. Just do what you can."

"I'm also going to put you on some strong antibiotics. It's infection you'll need to worry about at this point. Have you had a tetanus shot lately?"

"Two years ago."

"How's it going in here?" Dr. Sam Browning asked, sticking his head into the room.

"Okay. Just taking care of our hero here," Isaac answered.

"Don't say that. I'm no hero," Nate spat out.

Isaac paused in his suturing to regard Nate. "That's not what I've heard from the people that've come in and out of here all afternoon and evening. According to them, you kept your head."

Isaac sighed and went back to sewing. "You know I like you, right?"

Nate was confused by the question. "I guess so, why?"

"Because I need you to know that before I say what I'm about to say."

Nate gripped Rio's hand tighter. "Spit it out, Isaac."

"I didn't think you were the best man for the job. I like you, and I think you had the community's best interests at heart, but I wasn't sure you were what we needed to lead this town."

Nate swallowed around the lump in his throat. He'd been right. Despite winning the election, he didn't have the confidence of the people.

"I was wrong," Isaac stated.

"No, you weren't," Nate confessed. "I suck at the whole mayor thing."

"Quade was a great mayor, but he couldn't stand the sight of blood or even the thought of being around sick people. I'm not faulting him, it was just the way he was. How do you think he would've handled this tragedy?" Sam asked, stepping further into the room.

Nate rolled his eyes. "Well it's nice to know that if, God forbid, we ever have another tragedy, I'll be the best man to be mayor."

Isaac shook his head. "You're not listening. Every man brings something different to the table. For Quade, it was his business and engineering skills. You may not have those yet, but they can be learned. What can't be taught is compassion. And you, Mr. Mayor, have that in spades."

"And after what happened today, you're the perfect man to help heal this town," Sam added.

Nate was stunned by the vote of confidence he'd just been given. He felt his eyes begin to burn but quickly blinked away the tears. If he started crying again, he knew he wouldn't stop for days.

"Then get me fixed up and let me get back out there."

Isaac grinned. "A couple more and you'll be finished. Sam, why don't you fill out a prescription for Nate and give Rio a couple of samples until they can get them filled."

Sam gestured for Rio to follow him. Rio gave Nate's hand another squeeze before following the doctor into the hall.

"Casey's having a service at noon."

Isaac nodded. "I heard. Although, from the number of people talking about it, I doubt the church will be big enough."

Nate agreed. He wondered where they could hold a service. "Maybe we could hold it at the park."

Isaac finished tying off the last suture and cut the thread. "That might be the perfect spot."

They'd have to get all the chairs trucked over and set up, but Nate was sure there were plenty of people that would help. "Do you think it's too late to call Casey?"

Isaac shook his head and finished putting a sterile bandage on Nate's arm. "He's probably downtown with the others. You'll just have to find him."

"Done?"

"Yep. Just keep it clean and remember to take the entire prescription of antibiotics. If you notice heat or redness, give me a call or come in."

Nate shook Isaac's hand after getting to his feet. "Thanks for all you've done. I know this day wasn't easy for you either."

"I'll admit I was glad we were treating only minor cuts and scrapes. Physician or not, I don't know if I could've handled an entire day of seeing my friends come in with serious injuries."

"Yeah. Well, I'll see you tomorrow?" Nate asked as he walked into the hall.

"We'll be there."

* * * *

"Hey," Rawley greeted.

Ryan shut the door of his SUV and turned to find Rawley, Jeb, Garron and Sonny standing in front of him. The group of men looked completely worn out.

"How're things going?" Ryan asked, gesturing towards the crowd gathered at one end of the street.

"I don't know. We've done about everything we can do for them. It might be different if we knew 'em better, but we're seen as outsiders and rightly so." Rawley glanced over his shoulder. "I've never seen a closer bunch of people. You should be proud to be a part of this town."

"Believe me, I am. I witnessed the true spirit of Cattle Valley today." Ryan felt himself getting too emotional at the memory of the men and women pitching together to rescue their neighbours and friends.

Jeb stepped forward and wrapped his arms around Ryan. At first Ryan didn't know what to do. He knew he was already on the verge of breaking down, and he still needed to find his men and get them home. He finally settled on giving Jeb a quick hug back. "Thanks."

Jeb pulled back. "We're going back to the lodge for a couple of hours, but we'll be back first thing in the morning to help clean up and get the tables and chairs back to Sheridan for you."

Ryan nodded. "I'd appreciate that. I'm sorry things didn't go like we'd planned, but maybe you could come back next year. I'd bet it'll be the best Cattle Valley Days this town's ever seen."

"We were going to go home tomorrow, but we've talked about it and decided to stay until after the funeral services this week," Garron added.

"Thanks." Ryan hated the thought of burying men so young. "Maybe we could get together for another barbeque out at our place on Monday evening."

Garron nodded. "Just let us know." He pointed towards the parking lot. "Lilly, Ranger and Ryker are waiting in the Suburban, so I guess we'd best get. Nate and Rio are still working."

"Doesn't surprise me a bit." Ryan was so damn proud of his men he could burst.

After a round of handshakes and hugs, his friends walked off towards the parking lot and Ryan set off in the direction of the small crowd.

He found Rio and Nate serving coffee to a large group of people. "Hey," he greeted as he gave each of them a kiss.

"Any word from the inspector?" Nate asked.

Ryan shook his head. "He said he'd send the full report after he did some more investigating. I did get a bit of good news. Pam and the boys have been reunited. It seems after they got their popcorn, they snuck behind the barricades and were out by the bull pens when the collapse happened. One of the cowboys found them standing there and held on to them until someone came to claim them."

"Thank God they weren't where they were supposed to be," Nate said.

Ryan leaned over and whispered in Nate's ear. "What're all these people still doing here?"

Nate surveyed the crowd of around fifty people. "I don't know. Evidently they seem to be drawing some kind of strength from each other."

The new guy in town, Ethan, and Jay were passing out cookies. Ryan thought it was the most he'd ever seen Jay interact with people.

"He's been great," Nate said, evidently reading Ryan's mind again.

"At least he's not hiding in his apartment."

"I guess he's been out here since it happened. Luckily, he wasn't at the rodeo. He'd stayed home to watch Gracie so Hearn and Tyler could get the ball fields ready for tomorrow's tournament final."

Ryan was glad to hear his friends hadn't been at the rodeo. He noticed the dark circles under Nate and Rio's eyes. There was no doubt in his mind that he looked as tired as his men did. "Ready to head home?"

"What about these people?" Nate asked.

Ryan gathered Nate in his arms. "They'll lean on each other if they need to. We have long days ahead of us. There'll be plenty of things to do in the morning, but unless we get a little sleep, we won't be doing anyone any good. Besides, I need to personally inspect both my lovers' bodies for injuries."

"He's right," Rio said, stepping up to put his arms around both Ryan and Nate. "Let's call it a night and go home and take care of each other. I have a lot to be thankful for."

"We all do," Nate agreed. "Let me tell Jay and Sean we're leaving."

Ryan hadn't even noticed Sean. He watched Nate weave through the tables. Sean was sitting with his head propped in his hand, watching Ryan Bronwyn sleep. The antique store owner had a pretty large bandage on his forehead.

Nate bent over Sean and spoke into his ear. Sean nodded and said something back. Nate squeezed Sean's shoulder before making his way back through the area.

"I'm ready," Nate said.

"Why's Ryan asleep at the table? Why isn't he home?"

Nate glanced back over at the pair of men. "Sean doesn't know. He found him asleep earlier. He tried to wake him, but Ryan said he'd rather be here than home alone."

"So Sean's taken up the job of watching him sleep?"

Nate grinned. "I think today might bring a lot of people together."

"Hell. If we were a heterosexual community, we'd have a baby boom in nine and a half months."

Nate wrapped an arm around Ryan's waist. "Take me home."

"It'll be my pleasure."

* * * *

Rio was the first one up the following morning. He quietly got out of bed and made a pot of coffee. While he was waiting, he turned on the small television on the counter. It was the first time he'd caught the news since the previous day's events.

Sure enough, just as he'd feared, Cattle Valley was the main topic of discussion. From the air, the scene looked as bad as it had from the ground. The anchor woman told the viewers that four people had died and twenty-two still remained hospitalised, one in intensive care.

Rio's stomach dropped. Had Carol or Asa taken a turn for the worse? *Oh shit.* What if Ezra suffered another heart attack?

The segment ended with a shot of Nate looking over the rescue effort with tears in his eyes. *That picture says it all*, Rio thought.

The story on the collapse was quickly followed by news that business owner and billionaire, Asa Montgomery, was injured in the tragedy but was expected to recover. Rio breathed a sigh of relief. At least Mario would be happy.

He switched off the television and set the cups on a tray. After fixing three perfectly prepared cups of coffee, Rio carried them upstairs. He set the tray on the bedside table and crawled back in bed.

Rio snuggled up to Nate and pulled his lover against his chest. The dried cum on Nate's torso reminded Rio of the slow lovemaking of the previous night. Despite the fact they were all exhausted, they all felt the overwhelming need to physically love each other.

The tenderness Ryan displayed as he made love to him still caused a catch in his chest. Ryan was a lover with many facets and Rio enjoyed them all, but the incredible care his lover had taken with him was better than anything he'd ever experienced.

Rio felt Nate's long lashes tickle against his chest as the blinked. "Morning."

Nate scooted up and gave Rio a kiss. "Morning. Do I smell coffee?"

Rio grinned. "Made just the way you like it."

He reached over and picked up the cup, handing it to Nate.

"Mmmm, and served just the way I like it, too."

"Got one of those for me?" Ryan asked.

"Of course." Rio passed Ryan his morning brew.

Nate sat against the headboard. He seemed to be his old self for several moments. Rio knew the second Nate remembered the tragedy of the previous day.

"We should get going," Nate said.

"It's early. We have a few minutes." Rio took a sip of his own coffee.

Nate slurped his coffee making Rio and Ryan laugh.

"In a hurry?" Ryan asked.

Nate passed the empty mug back to Rio. "Yep. There are other things besides caffeine that get me going in the morning."

When Rio turned to put the cup back on its tray, Nate pounced on him. Surprised, Rio glanced over his shoulder. "What're you doing?"

Grinding his morning erection against Rio's ass, Nate chuckled. "What does it feel like I'm doing?"

Rio turned his head in the other direction and looked at Ryan. His lover's face mimicked his own shocked expression. Nate never, ever topped. What the hell was going on?

"You wanna fuck our Rio?" Ryan asked.

"Mmm hmm," Nate answered, reaching for lube.

Ryan's eyebrows rose as he gave Rio a shrug.

A slick finger teased against Rio's hole. It suddenly no longer mattered that Nate was acting completely out of character. Rio rose to his knees, making it easier for his baby to love him.

Ryan positioned himself against the headboard with a leg on either side of Rio's body. It didn't take a brain surgeon to know what his sheriff wanted. As Nate continued to finger his ass, Rio began to nuzzle Ryan's balls.

Ryan moaned and buried his fingers in Rio's hair.

Rio couldn't keep the grin from his face. His men sure did love to control him by his hair. God forbid he ever decide to get it cut. Hell. He'd probably be one of those old guys with long grey hair. Damn, he hated that look, too. Still, better to keep his men happy in the bedroom than worry about what he looked like to the general public.

He felt Nate kneel behind him and prepared himself to be fucked. He could tell by the quick jab of fingers in and out of his ass that Nate was getting himself worked up. "I'm ready," he told Nate.

Rio glanced up at Ryan and grinned. Ryan smiled back and directed Rio's mouth to his cock. "Pushy bastard."

Despite the token protest at his lover's forcefulness, Rio ate it up, both the attitude and the cock in front of him. The crown of Nate's cock breeched his hole. Rio tried to help his lover out by rocking back.

A sharp slap to his ass stopped him. "Hey!"

"Stay still. This is mine," Nate ordered.

Going back down on Ryan's cock, Rio glanced up and rolled his eyes. Between the slap to his ass, and Ryan's firm grip on his hair, he wondered what he'd gotten himself into.

Nate gripped Rio by the hips and surged inside in one hard thrust.

"Fuck," Rio said around the cock in his mouth. One of Ryan's hands released Rio's hair and travelled down to pull at his nipples.

Rio groaned. God, he loved nipple play. Behind him, Nate pulled back before pushing back inside. Each time Nate withdrew, the fucking grew more intense. Rio tickled Ryan's hole with one finger as he held the base of the heavily veined cock with the other.

Ryan began to move his legs. Rio wasn't sure what his lover was up to until he felt bare feet rubbing against his cock. It was like sensory overload. Rio jerked as his release seemed to come out of nowhere. He smiled at the thought of painting his partner's feet with his seed. That was definitely some kinky shit. Who knew that a pair of soft feet could set him off like that?

He was still pondering the question when he felt the first shot of Ryan's cum hit the back of his throat. He pulled back enough to taste the salty elixir that he loved.

Nate began fucking him like a man possessed, changing angles mid-stroke. As soon as the rhythm became erratic, Rio knew his lover was getting ready to fall over the edge. He slurped up the last of Ryan's seed and turned to glance over his shoulder.

"Give it to me, baby."

Nate gave a grunt to rival any of Ryan's as he came. Rio still didn't know what had come over Nate, but if this was the end result, he was just fine with the changes.

E p i l o g u e

One Month Later

"Have you seen this?" Ryan asked, holding up his magazine.

Rio set the free weights he'd been bench pressing in the cradle and sat up. He took the magazine from his lover's hand and whistled. "Holy Shit, Nate's gonna freak."

The front cover was the picture that had already been in the newspapers following the tragedy. The same shot Rio had seen on television the morning after the event, his beautiful Nate standing among the rubble with tears in his eyes. Only this time it was a glossy full page colour picture on the front of one of the biggest news magazines in the country. Rio admitted to himself that the photo still had the ability to choke him up. The expression of complete and utter despair on his partner's face was one Rio never wanted to see again. The headline splashed across the bottom of Nate's picture read, *A Private Community's Nightmare.*

"Check out page twenty-six."

Rio flipped to the indicated section and gasped. "Where'd they get these pictures?"

"I don't know. Either they snuck someone into the church service, or one of our own sold us out."

Rio's gaze once again went back to the spread of pictures. A few shots of the aftermath immediately following the collapse had already been printed in papers across the country. The photos that ate at Rio's insides were the ones of his friends' mourning the loss of four people they'd come to love.

He tossed the magazine to the floor. "That's gonna kill Nate."

"I know. So what are we gonna do about it?" Ryan asked.

"We could buy up every copy in town and hope he never hears about it?" Rio offered.

Ryan reached down and cupped Rio's cheek. "Shame on you. Have you already forgotten our promises to each other to always tell the truth, even when we know someone might get hurt?"

Rio hadn't forgotten, but Nate was finally starting to heal, along with many residents of Cattle Valley. But a promise was a promise. "Where's he at now? Because if he's going to find out, I'd rather it be from us."

"He should be at the office."

"Shit. Mario has a class in a half an hour. He's been so pissed off lately, I refuse to even think of telling the guy to cancel it."

"What's he pissed about?"

Rio shrugged. "He spent two days at the hospital waiting on word about Asa, but every time he asked to see him, Asa refused."

"Fuck. No wonder he's pissed. What the hell is Asa playing at?"

Rio shook his head. "I don't know. Maybe he didn't want Mario to see him helpless like that."

"That's screwed up. So what time?"

"Can you meet me there at noon?" Rio asked.

"Yeah. I have an interview set up at eleven, but I should be finished in plenty of time."

"Still haven't found someone to replace Rick?" Rio knew it wasn't the lack of good candidates applying. They'd probably had every gay cop in the nation apply for the one position available.

"No one will replace Rick," Ryan mumbled.

"I know you miss your friend, but it's time you and Roy stop working twelve-hour shifts seven days a week to make up for his loss."

With his hands on his hips, Ryan gazed out the window. "I know. Actually, I've been thinking about petitioning the city council to hire two deputies instead of just one."

"I hate to say it, but with an article like that one, you might need to think about adding more than two."

Ryan's gaze swung from the window back to Rio. "You think there'll be trouble?"

"Not necessarily, but I think our town has come out of the closet, so to speak. I imagine we'll get lovers and haters alike from now on."

"I hope to hell you're wrong about someone trying to use this to further hurt the people of this community." Ryan's jaw began clenching, which was never a good sign.

The last thing Rio wanted was to upset Ryan. "I'm just saying it might not be a bad idea to be prepared."

Although Ryan was still visibly tense, he nodded. "Agreed."

* * * *

Ryan waited for Rio on the steps of city hall. The interview he'd barely finished in time had gone well. The entire time he talked to the guy, Rio's words of warning continued to plague him.

"Hey," Rio greeted.

Ryan pushed off the side of the building and gave his lover a quick kiss. "You ready to do this?"

Rio held up the magazine Ryan had taken to him earlier. "I'm not ready, but I know it's the right thing to do."

Ryan opened the door and entered the building. He turned right and walked into Carol's office. It still seemed odd not to have the normal smart-ass woman ready with a comeback every time he came through the door.

According to her doctor, it would be at least another month before Carol could even think of returning to her old job. In the meantime, Nate had hired their newest resident, Ethan, to help out.

Ryan waved to Ethan as he strode through to Nate's office. His eyes immediately went to the magazine in the centre of his lover's desk.

"Um, Sheriff? He's not here," Ethan said, following them into the empty space.

"I see that. Where'd that come from?" he asked, pointing towards the magazine.

"It came in the mail. I guess the guy who wrote the article sent it to him," Ethan answered.

Ryan took a deep breath and closed his eyes. "How'd he take it?"

Ethan began to look flustered. "I don't know. I gave him the morning mail. He came out of his office about twenty minutes later and said he'd be back."

That didn't sound like the Nate he knew. "He didn't say anything else? No screaming? No throwing things?"

Ethan shook his head. "Like I said, he just left. I figured he must have a meeting or something."

Ryan looked at Rio. "Where would he go?"

"Home?" Rio offered.

Ryan shook his head. "If he were upset he'd have called us. This sounds more like pissed. You know how quiet he gets when he's really mad about something."

"So where would he go if he was pissed about that article?" Rio ran his hands through his hair. "You don't think he went back there, do you?"

"That's exactly what I think." Ryan turned on his heel and rushed out the door. The three of them had talked at length about what was going to happen to the rodeo grounds. The city council agreed with Nate that they needed to let some time pass before they made any decisions concerning the arena.

Ryan climbed into his SUV. As soon as Rio was in and buckled up, Ryan raced out of town. "What's he thinking?"

"Did you read the article?" Rio asked.

"What? No. I know what happened. I was there," Ryan snarled.

"I know you were. But in the article, the guy basically told readers how to get to the rodeo grounds. It was like he was sending them here to see the damage with their own eyes."

"Fuck!" Ryan growled as he punched his fist against the dash. As soon as they were out of town, he turned on the siren and pressed the gas pedal to the floor.

It took them mere minutes to arrive at the arena, or what was left of it. Sitting in the operator's seat of a city bulldozer, Nate ploughed through the concession stand.

"He's gonna kill himself," Rio yelled and jumped from the SUV before Ryan had a chance to put the vehicle in park.

Ryan threw the car in park and turned off the engine before racing after Rio. "Stop!" he said, wrapping his arms around Rio's waist.

"What?"

"Let him do this."

"You're as crazy as he is. He's not a heavy equipment operator. What if he gets hurt?"

Ryan looked at the determined face of his lover as he mowed down a section of the pens. "He's already hurt. Maybe this will help him heal."

"So we're just supposed to sit here and watch him?" Rio asked.

"Nope. We go get a couple of the big city trucks and help our mayor clean this place up."

Ryan caught a glimpse of the old sparkle in Nate's eyes and knew he was right. "Everything's gonna be just fine."

About the Author

An avid reader for years, one day Carol Lynne decided to write her own brand of erotic romance. Carol juggles between being a full-time mother and a full-time writer. These days, you can usually find Carol either cleaning jelly out of the carpet or nestled in her favourite chair writing steamy love scenes.

Carol loves to hear from readers. You can find her contact information, website details and author profile page at http://www.total-e-bound.com

Total-E-Bound Publishing

www.total-e-bound.com

Take a look at our exciting range of literagasmic™
erotic romance titles and discover pure quality
at Total-E-Bound.